# AUTOBIOGRAPHY
# WITHOUT WORDS

## Peter Cherches

*Autobiography Without Words* by Peter Cherches
ISBN-10: 1-938349-56-3
ISBN: 978-1-938349-56-0
eISBN: 978-1-938349-57-7
Library of Congress Control Number: 2016946746

Some of the pieces in this collection have appeared in the following journals, anthologies, and websites:

*Annandale Dream Gazette, Appearances, Black Scat Review, Contemporaries, Gargoyle, Grand Tour, Guys Write for Guys Read, Hambone, Little Star, Lost and Found: Stories from New York, Mr. Beller's Neighborhood, MungBeing, New Flash Fiction Review.*

Layout and Book Design by Mark Givens
cover photo by Elliot Schneider
author photo by Derek Berg

First Pelekinesis Printing 2017

For information:
Pelekinesis, 112 Harvard Ave #65, Claremont, CA 91711 USA

www.pelekinesis.com

# AUTOBIOGRAPHY WITHOUT WORDS

## PETER CHERCHES

# CONTENTS

*In memory of Barton Michael Cherches, 1944–2007, an icon in the insulation market.*

"This is the saddest story I have ever heard."

– Ford Madox Ford, *The Good Soldier*

"When I get nostalgic I read weather reports from my childhood."

– Peter Cherches, June 13, 2013

I plan to publish my autobiography without words. The book will consist solely of blank pages in white and black and shades of gray. It will open with a thin, translucent sheet of white paper. The sheets will gradually get thicker, and from ages three to six or seven the white sheets will be as bright as sunshine. Then a little gray begins to creep in, gradually but progressively, until around age 12 or 13, when the pages become a charcoal gray. Over the next few years the pages progress to black, a black as dark as deep night. Quite a number of these black pages. Too many of these black pages. But then the story takes a turn for the better. At the top of the pitch-black pages a little white, a little light, begins to creep in, and over the next several years of our tale the white eventually takes over the black. From there on, we have many, many pages of white, not always the brightest white, maybe, sometimes a little off-white, but still white. Then, toward the end of the book, the still-white pages become crumpled, but crumpled in an amusing way, the author hopes. Crumpled in a way, the author hopes, that will sum up the entire story.

# PART I

1964

Dear MOM I love you
very much, My Throat
hurts very much,
THE NIGHT OF Apr 14,
my throat almost
died IT HURTED
So MUch Please let
ME STAy HOME

LOVE PETER

# KIDS

While I was out for a walk one recent afternoon I saw a couple of kids on the street who reminded me of two of my childhood friends. Actually, they more than reminded me of my friends, they looked exactly like them. And they were wearing clothes that looked like mid-sixties styles. One of the kids had a small transistor radio to his ears. "Have you heard the rumor?" one of the boys said to the other.

"What's that?" his friend asked.

"Koufax is gonna retire," the first one said.

"Bullshit," replied the friend.

"No kidding," the first kid said. "They said it on the radio."

I pulled up closer to them and could hear the radio. Music was playing. It was "Summer in the City," by the Lovin' Spoonful. Must be an oldies station, I figured.

Next thing I knew, one of the kids turned to me. "You know," he said, "you look just like our friend Peter." Then he added, "If he was an old bald guy, that is."

# Young Peter Cherches, a Film by Martin Scorsese

I was thrilled, of course, when Scorsese's people contacted me to tell me that Marty wanted to make a film about an incident in my childhood, and that he was prepared to pay handsomely for the rights. And, though the contract didn't give me any say over casting, Marty was thoughtful enough to introduce me to the young actor who'd be playing me in the film. We had arranged to meet at Bar Pitti, in The Village, at one of the outdoor tables. I was the first to arrive, and I ordered a glass of Vermentino to sip while waiting. Marty and the kid showed up about ten minutes later. The kid looked to be about eight, the age I was when the events of the film take place.

I must say I was rather disturbed that the kid was wearing a yarmulke. He didn't look Jewish, though. As a matter of fact, he was blond with a little goyish nose and looked a lot like Jay North, from "Dennis the Menace." Hmm, an orthodox kid who looks like a gentile, I thought, this has possibilities. Still, I couldn't make peace with the yarmulke.

"There's a problem," I told Scorsese. "I didn't wear a yarmulke as a kid."

"Don't worry," Marty replied. "We can shoot around it."

Now when I was a kid I had dirty-blond hair and I didn't look particularly Jewish. And my family was totally secular; we never went to synagogue. I did, however, have a bar mitzvah, which was essentially a secular ritual, an excuse for a party, all religious trappings aside. It was, in fact, during my quickie bar mitzvah lessons with Mrs. Goldstein, our local Evelyn Wood of painless haftorah prep, that I became a resolute atheist, too late, alas, to cancel the big event at Leonard's of Great Neck. So you can understand why I was apprehensive about being played by a kid in a yarmulke.

But I did want to give the kid a chance, so I started chatting with him. He turned out to be incredibly bright, charming and witty—he reminded me of myself as a kid. I was starting to like him. Still, the religion thing was something I was having trouble making peace with. I knew I wouldn't be able to get him to renounce Judaism, but I figured if I could at least get him to scoff at other religions I'd be somewhat placated and we could put our differences aside.

"All right, you're an orthodox Jew," I said, "so I guess that means you believe in God. But I'll bet you think all other religions are pretty ridiculous, right?"

"Not at all," the kid replied. "I think there's much to admire in all the world's religions. In fact, I think we should all try to emulate Jesus Christ."

Oy vey, this is not going to work, I thought. As much as I liked the kid, I was sure he didn't possess the requisite irreverence to pull off a convincing portrayal of me as an eight-year-old, especially considering the nature of the events at the heart of the story.

When the kid went inside to go to the bathroom, I expressed my doubts to Marty. "He's a good kid," I said, "but he just doesn't seem right for the part."

"Don't worry, Pete," Marty said. "This kid is good. Real good. Talented beyond his years. You just wait and see. I think you'll be thrilled when the project is finished."

Well, like I said, my contract doesn't include any say over casting, so I left it at that. The kid came back, we finished our drinks and our meeting, shook hands and went our separate ways.

Shooting starts in about a month, and I'm told the film should hit the theatres sometime next year. I hope Marty's right about the kid.

# MY:EARLIEST:MEMORY

I:DON'T:REMEMBER:MY:FATHER:HE:DIED:
WHEN:I:WAS:TWO:YEARS:OLD:HOWEVER:IT:
STRUCK:ME:RECENTLY:THAT:MY:EARLIEST:
MEMORY:HAS:TO:DO:WITH:THE:REALIZATION:
THAT:MY:FATHER:HAD:DIED:IT:WAS:SHORTLY:
AFTER:HE:MY:FATHER:HARRY:CHERCHES:
HAD:DIED:OF:LEUKEMIA:IN:1958:AND:THIS:
MEMORY:TAKES:PLACE:SEVERAL:MONTHS:
MAYBE:A:YEAR:LATER:AND:IT'S:ACTUALLY:A:
PRETTY:MOVING:STORY:AND:IN:A:SENSE:IT:
ALSO:HAS:TO:DO:WITH:MOVING:YOU:SEE:
WHEN:MY:FATHER:WAS:ALIVE:WE:HAD:TWO:
ADJOINING:APARTMENTS:THE:SMALLER:ONE:
HAD:MY:BEDROOM:AND:MY:PARENTS':
BEDROOM:AND:THE:LARGER:APARTMENT:
HAD:THE:LIVING:ROOM:MY:BROTHERS':
BEDROOM:AND:THE:DEN:AND:MY:EARLIEST:
MEMORY:HAS:TO:DO:WITH:THESE:TWO:
APARTMENTS:AND:RALPH:RALPH:WAS:A:
CONTRACTOR:HE:WAS:CLOSING:UP:THE:
ENTRANCE:BETWEEN:THE:TWO:APARTMENTS:
THE:ENTRANCE:LED:FROM:THE:FOYER:OF:
THE:LARGER:APARTMENT:WE:ALWAYS:SAID:

FOY-ER:NOT:FWA-YEA:INTO:THE:LIVING:
ROOM:OF:THE:SMALLER:APARTMENT:WHICH:
AT:THE:TIME:WAS:MY:PARENTS':ROOM:OR:
SHOULD:I:SAY:MY:MOTHER'S:ROOM:SINCE:MY:
FATHER:WAS:DEAD:AND:RALPH:WAS:CLOSING:
UP:THE:ENTRANCE:WITH:PLASTERBOARD:
AND:I:REMEMBER:I:WAS:WATCHING:RALPH:
AND:MY:MOTHER:WAS:THERE:AND:MY:AUNT:
NORMA:TOO:AND:I:KNEW:SOMETHING:WAS:
GOING:ON:BUT:IT:REALLY:DIDN'T:HIT:ME:
WHAT:BUT:OF:COURSE:WHAT:WAS:HAPPENING:
WAS:THAT:WE:WERE:GETTING:RID:OF:ONE:OF:
THE:APARTMENTS:BECAUSE:WE:REALLY:
DIDN'T:NEED:IT:ANYMORE:OR:BECAUSE:WE:
COULDN'T:AFFORD:IT:AND:I:REMEMBER:
RALPH:WAS:A:VERY:FRIENDLY:GUY:I:LIKED:
RALPH:BUT:I:SUPPOSE:I:HAD:A:TREMENDOUS:
FEELING:OF:ANXIETY:BECAUSE:I:KNEW:
SOMETHING:WAS:CHANGING:AND:THEN:I:
REMEMBER:I:WAS:STANDING:IN:THE:FOYER:
OF:THE:LARGER:APARTMENT:WATCHING:
RALPH:AND:I:HAD:TO:GO:TO:THE:BATHROOM:
AND:I:TOLD:MY:MOTHER:AND:I:STARTED:
WALKING:TO:THE:FRONT:DOOR:OF:THE:
LARGER:APARTMENT:WHICH:BY:THE:WAY:WAS:
1D:THE:SMALLER:ONE:WAS:1C:AND:I:GUESS:I:
WENT:FOR:THE:FRONT:DOOR:BECAUSE:RALPH:
WAS:CLOSING:UP:THE:PASSAGE:BETWEEN:THE:
TWO:APARTMENTS:AND:I:WANTED:TO:GET:
INTO:THE:SMALLER:APARTMENT:BECAUSE:

THAT:WAS:WHERE:MY:BATHROOM:WAS:BUT:
MY:MOTHER:TOLD:ME:TO:USE:THE:
BATHROOM:IN:THE:LARGER:APARTMENT:
BECAUSE:THE:SMALLER:ONE:WASN'T:OURS:
ANYMORE:AND:I:STARTED:THROWING:A:
TANTRUM:BECAUSE:I:WANTED:TO:USE:MY:
BATHROOM:AND:MY:AUNT:WAS:TRYING:TO:
CALM:ME:DOWN:TRYING:TO:EXPLAIN:WHILE:
MY:MOTHER:WAS:PUTTING:THE:TRAINING:
SEAT:ON:THE:TOILET:IN:1D:AND:I:KEPT:
INSISTING:THAT:I:DIDN'T:WANT:TO:USE:THAT:
TOILET:I:WANTED:TO:USE:MY:OWN:
BATHROOM:BUT:I:DID:HAVE:TO:"GO":REAL:
BAD:SO:I:FINALLY:GAVE:IN:AND:SAT:ON:THAT:
TOILET:AND:I:REMEMBER:I:WAS:CRYING:THE:
WHOLE:TIME:I:WAS:ON:THE:TOILET:AND:
THEN:I:CALLED:MY:MOTHER:IN:TO:WIPE:ME:
AND:I:WAS:STILL:CRYING:AND:I:GUESS:
THAT'S:WHEN:IT:REALLY:SUNK:IN:THAT:
SOMETHING:HAD:CHANGED:DRASTICALLY:
THAT:MY:FATHER:HAD:DIED:AND:I:ALSO:
REMEMBER:THAT:FOR:MANY:YEARS:TO:COME:I:
WOULD:OCCASIONALLY:KNOCK:ON:THE:
WALL:IN:THE:FOYER:OF:OUR:APARTMENT:
AND:YOU:COULD:HEAR:WHERE:THE:BRICK:
ENDED:AND:THE:PLASTERBOARD:STARTED:
AND:THAT:WAS:WHERE:THE:ENTRANCE:WAS:
WHEN:WE:HAD:TWO:APARTMENTS:

# A Gift from My Father

One of the few things my father had a chance to give me, before he died in my third year on this earth, was a nickname. Though the moniker didn't stick, when I was very young I was sometimes called Pumpie—a diminutive of Peter Peter Pumpkin Eater. I don't think I was ever called Pumpie after the age of five.

I'm not sure what it is, but there's something I envy about people who have nicknames. Maybe it's the feeling that you can get closer to a person through a nickname, less formal and all that. I guess that's why, sometime in my twenties, I started introducing myself as Pete instead of Peter. I've never had a nickname that stuck (for a short while my brothers called me Fat Pete, but thankfully that never really caught on), and I recently thought about trying to revive Pumpie. But I quickly discarded the idea. To my ears the name Pumpie sounds sort of WASPish, preppy, certainly not appropriate to the Pete Cherches of today. I guess a nickname has to be earned, or at least grown into. Perhaps if I were called Pumpie all along it would fit now—and I'd probably be a somewhat different person as a result. I guess that wasn't meant to be, so now I just keep it in my scrapbook of memory. And since it's one of the few gifts I have from my father, I occasionally take it out and say it, out loud. Pumpie.

# NEW DADDY WITH A
# MUSTACHE

My mother remarried about four years after my father died, when I was six. In the interim, while I was fatherless, I had hoped my mother would marry a man with a mustache. I'm pretty sure this interest in mustaches had to do with Herbie. Herbie was a sort of father surrogate, but unattainable, I knew, as a real father. He was a friend of the family and the husband of my mother's friend Penny, who owned a women's clothing store, Penny's Little Shop. Dark and mustachioed, Herbie had a kind of Latin lover look about him, though he was Jewish. Herbie spent a lot of time at our house because he drove for a limousine service and often had time off during the day while his wife was at the store. Herbie used to come over to dance the cha cha cha with my mother. I even remember one of the records, "Tea for Two" with a Latin beat. I liked Herbie a lot, but since he was unavailable I went looking for mustachioed fathers elsewhere.

Whenever I was out with my mother and saw a man with a mustache, any man with a mustache, I would go up to him and ask, "Will you be my new daddy with a mustache?"

My mother found this very embarrassing. "You'd ask anyone with a mustache," she told me years later, "young men, old men, store owners, construction workers. I remember, we were once in a cab and you asked the driver if he'd be your new daddy with a mustache. A schvartzer!"

My mother remarried in 1962, when I was six years old, thereby sparing herself further embarrassment. My stepfather didn't have a mustache, but he did have a very big nose.

I visited my mother, a widow again, in Florida and in her eighties, and decided to ask her about a suspicion I'd always had.

"Were you having an affair with Herbie?" I asked her.

"No," she replied. "He was a good-looking guy, but he wasn't my type." Then she added, "I think he drove for the mob."

# Miss Coney Island

## I

Stand up straight... Milton Berle?... How do you remember?—You're really something... I don't remember. Miss Venus? That sounds right. Do you remember everything I ever told you?... No, I won't let you tape this. I know you. You'll only make fun of me... Well, looking back, I'll tell you something, I felt cheap. Like meat on display... Well, I wasn't really Miss Coney Island of 1940—I mean, they had them every month. I was August and your Aunt Norma was September... All right, I was Miss Coney Island of August 1940... What talent? All it was was bathing suits. You'd parade around in a bathing suit and they'd pick a winner... Nervous? I guess so... The Loew's Coney Island Theater. They had the contests at the Saturday matinee. It was all part of the show. They'd show a couple of shorts, maybe The Three Stooges, Flash Gordon, a couple of movies, and somewhere in the middle was the beauty contest, and one month I won, and Norma won the next... Shirley? No, she wasn't so attractive. This was before the nose job... Well, a couple of others. I don't think I ever really thought I'd be Miss America. Don't forget, this was before Bess Myerson... I think Miss Venus was a preliminary for a preliminary for Miss New York... Right, and Milton Berle was the judge, and afterwards he came up to me and said, "Honey, if it wasn't for your posture you would have had it in the bag." And that's why I always tell you to stand up straight... So stand up straight... And don't make a story out of this.

## II

My mother was a nickel and dime beauty queen. Miss Coney Island of 1940—August 1940, that is. You see, they held these beauty contests once a month at the Loew's Coney Island movie theater, during the Saturday matinee. This was back in the days when a Saturday at the movies was an all-day affair—a double feature, some shorts, a serial and a beauty contest. So there's my mother, smack in the middle of Flash Gordon and maybe a Bette Davis film, on stage in a bathing suit. Now this was a real rudimentary beauty contest—no talent show, no evening gowns, no Miss Congeniality, just a bunch of teenage girls from Brooklyn in bathing suits. My mother won one month and my Aunt Norma won the next month. But my mother got the idea she should go on to bigger and better beauty contests. I'm not sure how many of these she entered, but the last one, I think, was called Miss Venus, and it was supposed to be one of the preliminaries for Miss New York State, itself a preliminary for Miss America. I don't think my mother had any illusions of becoming Miss America— after all, this was before Bess Myerson became the first Jewish Miss America. But my mother had been bitten by the beauty contest bug—until Milton Berle came along and rained on her parade, that is. Uncle Miltie was the judge of the Miss Venus pageant. I don't think this one was much more elaborate than Miss Coney Island— mostly prancing around in bathing suits. My mother's prancing, unfortunately, was marred by a fatal flaw— bad posture. She's fond of telling how Uncle Miltie came up to her after the contest was over and said, "Honey, if it wasn't for your posture you would have had it in the bag." She'd always tell this anecdote when she reminded me to correct my own posture. "If I had better posture I might have become Miss America. Who knows?" she'd say.

### III

### TAMARAC WOMAN WAS MISS AMERICA HOPEFUL

Tamarac, Florida, October 23, 1989; special to The Tattler — Sources reveal that Mrs. Edith Pike of The Pines at Woodmont once hoped to become the first Jewish Miss America. The Tattler has learned that Mrs. Pike, the former Edith Posner, entered a series of beauty pageants in her native Brooklyn, New York in the summer and fall of 1940. Mrs. Pike's career began with the Miss Coney Island contest, a monthly event sponsored by the Loew's Coney Island movie theater. She was the recipient of the August 1940 Miss Coney Island crown. The subsequent presentation of the September crown to Mrs. Pike's sister Norma, along with the fact that the pageant consisted of nothing more than a swimsuit competition wedged-in between a Flash Gordon episode and the second half of a double feature had some Brooklyn residents clamoring for an investigation.

According to Norma Kornreich, Mrs. Pike's sister and a resident of nearby Sunrise, "I was content to rest on my laurels, but Edie wanted to go on to bigger and better things. She may not admit it, but I think she really wanted to be the first Jewish Miss America." That honor, however, eluded Mrs. Pike. Shortly after the August Miss Coney Island victory, Mrs. Pike's career was cut short in an unsuccessful bid for the title of Miss Venus, an early preliminary for the Miss America pageant. Comedian Milton Berle, the judge for the contest, eliminated Mrs. Pike for bad posture, telling her afterwards, "Sweetheart, if it wasn't for your lousy posture you would have had it all sewn up." The distinction of being the first Jewish Miss America fell upon Bess Myerson several years later, just after World War II.

Mrs. Pike is still bitter about the Miss Venus experience. "It's all Milton Berle's fault," says the 65-year-old blonde. "He said it was because of my posture, but I think he must have had something against me. Maybe I didn't have the best posture in the world, but I had plenty of other things going for me. Who knows, if it wasn't for Milton Berle I just might have become the first Jewish Miss America."

Mr. Berle could not be reached for comment.

# THE TASTE OF IVORY

I don't remember what I said, but I remember her chasing me around the apartment with the big white bar in her hand, that crazed look in her eyes. I remember her catching me, grabbing me by the hair, trying to pry my jaws open, her long red nails scratching my face. I remember that the bar was too big for my little mouth, and I remember her turning it forty-five degrees so the corner could at least graze my tongue and make me gag. I remember the taste of Ivory soap.

# A Certain Document

The object of my investigation is a certain document, the writing at the edges obliterated by a mother's kiss. However, if there is no objection, I will first attempt to document my mother, a woman on the edge, before the wet kiss of necessity obliterates me. Of the object, the document, I'll say more in due time, of its edges in particular, but first I must obliterate the question of my mother, conjure an image in order to kiss it goodbye.

My mother was the object of my affection in the early days, and I constantly sought, in vain, her kisses, documentation of maternal love, as it were, a device to obliterate fear at the edges of infancy. She loved soap operas, my mother did, especially "The Edge of Night," often citing its ability to simultaneously document and objectify passion, giving a simple kiss, for instance, the power to obliterate a housewife's boredom. For thirty minutes a day the program had my mother on the edge of her seat, and any attempt to obliterate her concentration would turn her into a monster, her violent objections to my continual requests for kisses well documented by my resultant welts and bruises. An edgy woman, to be sure, my mother would try to obliterate my emotional scars with peace offerings, an object of the toy family, for instance, or a document of the genre "children's book," surrogate kisses from the marketplace. All this by way of explaining my mother and the role she may very well have played in the matter at hand, the object of the present discussion, the case of the document whose edges were obliterated by what appears, by all accounts, to have been a kiss.

What role my mother did play in this highly objectionable event, now known as "the affair of the document with the kissed off edges," is unclear, however, as much important evidence has been obliterated by the ravages of time, including my mother's ultimate dementia. What we do know for sure is that the words on the edges of said document were clearly obliterated by a combination of saliva and lipstick determined by exhaustive chemical analyses to be the by-products of a mother's kiss, though the identity of the guilty mother must perforce be the object of pure speculation. If I choose to believe it was my own mother whose kiss was responsible for the obliteration of the text at the edges of the document in question, it is no doubt out of a need to believe that she was indeed capable of such an act, capable of kissing something, that is, even if only an inanimate object.

# A Bus Ride

I rarely take buses in Brooklyn. The bus always seems to take so long compared to the subway. But, even though it only runs about every half hour, the B69 bus is the most direct way to get from Park Slope to Clinton Hill. The bus stop is just across the street from my building, but I still go down about ten minutes before the scheduled arrival time, just to be sure. I mean, those listed times are just guidelines. I don't think buses wait around if they're early.

Anyway, the bus was about five minutes late this time. It went up Seventh Avenue to Flatbush, then took a right toward Grand Army Plaza. The next thing I knew, we were in a tunnel. I was confused. I was unaware of a tunnel anywhere near Grand Army Plaza. It was a pretty long tunnel too, like the Lincoln. Not only was I confused, I was claustrophobic. I always hated tunnels when I was a kid, probably the first manifestation of my mild claustrophobia. The Lincoln Tunnel was the worst part of visits to my uncle Buddy in New Jersey.

So, we were driving through this mysterious tunnel for quite some time, and I was a little anxious, a bit short of breath, minor heart palpitations. Perhaps the tunnel's a shortcut, I thought.

When we finally exited the tunnel we were in familiar territory. Unfortunately. I say unfortunately because the route should have been through Prospect Heights and Fort Greene, but instead we were in Midwood, the neighborhood I grew up in. And then the P.A. came on.

It turned out I was on a tour bus. How this happened, I have no idea. But there was a tour guide with a microphone. "Here is the Kent Theater," the guide said, as we drove down Coney Island Avenue, between Avenues H and I. "This is where Peter Cherches went to matinees as a child."

She was talking about me! It turned out, I was to learn, that it was a tour of notable sites of my youth, in my old neighborhood. "There's a funny story about young Peter. Back in the sixties, it was not uncommon for unaccompanied children to go to neighborhood movie theaters. And one day, when Peter was home from school for a Jewish holiday, he decided to go to the movies because he thought the film they were showing would be fun for a kid. It was called *Toys in the Attic*, but Peter didn't understand a thing that was going on. You see, the film was a very adult melodrama, based on a play by Lillian Hellman."

She was right. Wow, I had completely forgotten about that! And I also completely forgot about the event I was headed to in Clinton Hill as I enjoyed the rest of the tour. When we returned to Park Slope I tipped the guide generously.

# The Old Neighborhood

A beautiful spring day, 1990. Patti wanted to see where I grew up, so I told her I'd take her on a walking tour of the old neighborhood. I hadn't been back for some years. One side of me was glad for the opportunity to go back and tell tales of my Brooklyn youth to someone from a foreign culture (Patti is a WASP from rural Pennsylvania), but another side of me was petrified—I had a miserable childhood, some horrible memories, and now I was returning to the scene of the crime. Oh well, I thought, at worst it will be a therapeutic experience.

We took the D train to Newkirk. We walked down to Coney Island Avenue and I showed Patti my grade school, P.S. 217. Then we walked toward Avenue H.

I told Patti about some colorful characters from the neighborhood. I told her about the guy who slept all day and rode the D train all night, and who once had a job as a commission salesman on the graveyard shift at an all-night men's clothing store—Dennison Clothes: "Money talks, nobody walks." I told her about the fat guy who went off the deep end, picked up a rifle and started taking pot shots out his window on Avenue H. And I told her about the guy who had become a psychologist and was arrested for sodomizing his patients at Creedmoor.

Kirschenbaum's funeral parlor was still at the corner of Avenue H and Coney Island Avenue. I remember hearing, when I was a kid, that Kirschenbaum was related to one of the Americans—one of Jay and the Americans, that is, and when you're a kid in the sixties that kind of connection is very exciting. Equally exciting was the news that Mary Tyler Moore had attended the local Catholic school, St. Rose of Lima. We all pronounced Lima like the bean.

Patti and I walked down Avenue H to my block, East 9th Street. I lived near the dead end, by the freight tracks. I looked down the street. The distance to the dead end seemed much shorter than I remembered.

We walked down the street. My heart started beating faster. Would I run into anybody I knew?

We got to my building.

We stood outside and stared at the entrance.

"Let's go in," Patti said.

"I don't know," I said. "What if we ran into somebody I know?"

"What would be so bad about that?" she asked.

"I might have to talk to them."

I finally decided to go in.

We read the directory. At a least a third of the names were familiar, people who had been there since my childhood, some of them for more than fifty years— nobody gives up a rent-controlled apartment. Ocasio, the super, was still there. Browner and Kurland were still there. Forman was still there. And Fergo was still there. Fergo, arch-enemy of all the kids on the block. Her name was Josephine Fergo, but to us she was just plain Fergo. She was an old Italian woman who dyed her hair red and wore lots of makeup. She used to scream at us when we played ball near her window. We screamed back. Sometimes she would throw hot water on an especially persistent kid. Fergo was a witch.

Fergo used to terrorize her husband, John. They would fight every Saturday morning, and he would spend the rest of the day in a lawn chair in front of the building, sulking. My mother told me that Fergo was a neat freak and that John had to take all his meals over the sink. We usually avoided Fergo's apartment on Halloween, but one year we decided to give her a try. Fergo gave each and every one of us one walnut, in the shell.

Patti and I left the building and started walking down the block. About halfway between the dead end and Avenue H we passed an old woman with dyed red hair. I looked at her. Did she recognize me? As soon as the woman was safely past us I said to Patti, in a stage whisper, "That was Fergo!"

The Fergo incident really impressed Patti. That evening we were dining at a Russian restaurant in Brighton Beach and Patti kept repeating, "What a day. What a day. We saw Fergo!"

# WHERE WAS I?

I was in Mrs. Dubron's second-grade class, and Mrs. Kandel, from the class next door, came in to make the announcement. These many years later I still remember that when Mrs. Kandel told us what had happened almost all of the girls started crying, but none of the boys did. We all went home early that day.

Though this may seem callous in retrospect, I was, after all, a kid, and I remember being most upset that I couldn't watch "The Flintstones" because it was pre-empted. "Pre-empted" was a word I learned from the TV Guide—that and "approximate," as in "time approximate after baseball." I also remember that my mother, who always knew which famous people were Jewish, told me that Jack Ruby was Jewish.

# Olde English Surnames

Back then, grown Jewish men had names like Irving and Morris and Seymour, names that have subsequently fallen into decades of disuse. My stepfather's name was Seymour, though he preferred to be called Sy.

When I was about seven I asked Sy where the name Seymour came from.

"It's an old English surname," he told me.

I thought he was pulling my leg. You see, I had never heard that fancy word for "last name" before. So, thinking of Lancelot and Galahad, and unable to imagine a Jew in shining armor, I said, "You're kidding! There was no Sir Seymour!"

# THE FUNNY COMPANY

Morty Gunty grew up in my neighborhood. A second (or third) string standup comic, Gunty played himself in Woody Allen's film *Broadway Danny Rose* (both Morty and Woody went to my high school, Midwood). Perhaps his greatest exposure was as the backup host for the Cerebal Palsy Telethon. Whenever Dennis James or Steve and Eydie needed a break in the wee hours, Morty would take over.

In 1964, when I was eight, Morty hosted a kids' show called "The Funny Company." Morty was long-gone from the neighborhood by that time, but his mother still lived around the corner from us, and she and my mother went to the same beauty parlor. So one day my mother said to Morty's mother, "Can your son get my son on his show?" Mother Gunty brokered the deal.

I can't remember whether the show was live or on tape, but I know I was in the studio on a Monday. I know this because my mother insisted I get a haircut before the show, and my regular barbershop (inside of which hung a photo of me getting my first haircut) was closed on Mondays. So my mother took me to Al's Barbershop for my haircut. It was the only time I went to Al's, but many years later, when I was living in the East Village, I went to the Astor Place Barbershop for a haircut, and the guy who was cutting my hair looked very familiar. I took a look at his license. Al Rizza. He had given up his shop in Brooklyn for a chair at Astor Place.

Anyway, sufficiently shorn to my mother's satisfaction, we headed to New York (as Brooklynites referred to Manhattan back then), for WOR studios. I was part of "the clubhouse" on Morty's show, the equivalent of the peanut gallery. A group of kids would talk with Morty and tell jokes between cartoons. I think there were maybe six of us in the clubhouse, and for some reason I remember the last name of one chubby kid—Pfeffer. It stuck with me. The oddest things stick with me. Years later I had a gastroenterologist named Pfeffer. When I saw him the first time he pronounced my last name correctly. When I noted this he said, "When you have a name like Pfeffer you make an effort."

Now as a kid I was pretty outgoing, a natural performer, but on "The Funny Company" I blew it. For some reason I froze up. Every time I was asked a question my monosyllabic answers were punctuated by Ralph Kramdenesque hum-a-na-hum-a-nas. On top of that, every time the camera panned to me I was scratching my back, because it was so itchy from the haircut.

All the kids on the show were asked to bring one joke to tell. This was the heyday of the moron joke, and I got mine from a book of moron jokes.

"Why did the moron take a bag of oats to bed with him?"

"I don't know, why did the moron take a bag of oats to bed with him?"

"So he could feed his nightmares!"

# Halloween Story

I think this happened when I was eight or nine, so it would have been 1964 or '65. That year I had my best costume ever. In one of the closets of our apartment I found a New York Giants baseball uniform that one of my older brothers had from the fifties. But I had a perverse imagination even at that age, and it wasn't enough for me to go as a baseball player. I decided to wear a skeleton mask too and claim I was the ghost of one of the dead Giants. I asked my brothers to give me the names of famous dead baseball Giants. I settled on Mel Ott.

My friends and I were power trick-or-treaters. These were the days when it was safe to go around ringing doorbells without parental escorts. A group of five or six of us would go around to a bunch of the six-story buildings in the neighborhood, starting at the top and working our way down, ringing every bell. Our takes were prodigious.

Occasionally, one of the adults would ask, "Who are you?" Sometimes I replied, "The ghost of Mel Ott," and sometimes just, "Mel Ott."

That year, at the end of the night, my shopping bag

was fuller and heavier than ever before. I was thrilled. I got home and boasted to my mother of my haul. I left the bag on the kitchen counter and went to sleep.

The next morning I ran into the kitchen, ready to start working my way through the Halloween candy, but the bag was gone. What could have happened? I figured one of my brothers must have taken it. But they were eight and twelve years older than me. I knew they wouldn't have stolen it, but maybe they hid it, as a joke. Both brothers, however, denied any part in the candy's disappearance.

I went over the apartment with a fine-tooth comb. I looked in every closet, every drawer, every cabinet, and under every bed, but the bag was nowhere to be found. It remained an unsolved mystery for weeks. After a while I pretty much forgot it.

A little after this, my brother Bart got a major fright when he went to the bathroom one night and saw a giant rat drinking out of the toilet. This rat was as big as a cat, he said. At first my mother wouldn't believe him. "This is no tenement," she said.

But soon there were other sightings and evidence. So my mother went out and bought mouse traps. That's right, mouse traps; little mouse traps. And she placed a little square of kosher salami in each of them, perhaps assuming a rat in a Jewish neighborhood would have Jewish tastes. In the morning the salami would be gone, the trap sprung, and the rat nowhere in sight.

Finally she realized she had to call Manny the super in to investigate. Manny moved the refrigerator out from its alcove. Behind the refrigerator was a big hole, leading down to the basement (we lived on the first floor). Also behind the refrigerator was my Halloween shopping bag, ripped to shreds, with only a subset of the original contents remaining, Milky Ways and Hershey Bars half-eaten, with big rat's teeth marks through the wrappers.

# GROWNUP PARTY

Scotch on the rocks, mostly, though a few sip "perfect" Manhattans, and there is that one uncle who always asks for "Cherry Herring." Cold cuts and canapés and cole slaw and potato salad. The cacophony of drunken conversation swells. A sloshed Ann Kalman, zaftig and bubbly in a Shelly Winters sort of way, loudly blurts out something about her vagina, shocks and excites the little pitcher with big ears. Jews dance the cha cha cha.

# A Fat Boy Remembers

My mother was a canasta maven. She played two or three times a week. I was always happy when the floating game was held at our apartment, because that meant there would be plenty of candy. I was a fat little boy, and my gluttony knew no bounds. My mother would leave out dishes of fruit and all sorts of candy. I didn't touch the fruit, but I ate about half the candy. My favorite was the bridge mix, chocolates with five or six different artificial centers. Every time I would go back for more candy, my mother would say, in front of all the canasta ladies, "Enough already! Aren't you fat enough?" It was embarrassing, but not enough to stop me.

*     *     *

I remember an ad that always used to run in the *Sunday Times Magazine*. It was an ad for a fat boys' camp, and it featured a photograph of a now svelte boy in a pair of oversized pants. The boy held the waist out to show how much weight he'd lost. Sometimes I would stand in front of a mirror and hold my stomach in and try to hold my pants out like the boy in the photo, but it hardly made a difference.

*     *     *

Every time I hear the word "tit," I think of what Lynn Kurland said to me in 1967. It was summertime, and we were both eleven. It must have been very hot out, as I had my shirt off, and I was normally loath to show off my chubby little body. So there we were, Lynn and I, girl and boy, puberty only a stone's throw away, when Lynn looked at me and said, "Boy, look at those tits! They're bigger than mine." And indeed they were.

Dear mom
I cant find my trunk key
I Didn't get sick on the bus
I Dont like it as much as
skymount.
I want to come
home.
My counselors names
are chuck and Mickey

love Peter

THIS LETTER IS TRUE

Dear mom and dad
I am having a bad time
I still think the
I said in my last things
I sent you are true letter
please do the thing i told
you in the last letter
I found the key for my
trunk.
            Love Peter

Dear Mom and Dad
I am having the same
kind of time
The boys in my bunks
names are Eric Barry
Gary and Bob

Dear Harvey and Barton,
If you dont know what
kind of time I am
having ask mom
I hope you are having
a nice summer
         Love Peter
P.S. I made a mistake on my
                     Letter to Young

# SABLE

In my childhood I was a hypochondriac, a psychosomatic wreck. I always had some complaint or other, and my family called me "the boy who cried wolf."

One Sunday afternoon, when I was about ten, I began to feel chest pains. "Call a doctor," I screamed, "I'm having a heart attack." But my mother told me to calm down, that it would go away. It didn't go away, and within an hour my hands, feet and face had blown up to twice their size. My face was flushed and I had broken out in hives all over my body. I was a grotesque apparition. So the doctor was called after all. When he came he gave me an injection and explained that I was having an extreme allergic reaction. Had I eaten anything new that day? We thought about it and remembered that at breakfast I had tried sable (smoked black cod) for the first time. It must have been the sable. At any rate, the injection worked and I was back to normal later that evening. My mother rewarded me by telling me I could stay home from school the next day.

One Sunday, a year or two later, I was feeling especially anxious and apprehensive about returning to school after the weekend. I always hated school, but this particular time there must have been something especially frightening, perhaps an oral presentation, or a dance festival. So that afternoon, while I was home alone, I went out to the local "appetizing" store, the Bagel 'N' Lox, and spent my allowance on a quarter pound of sable and an onion bagel. I rushed home and made a sandwich. I stared at it for several minutes. My heart started beating faster in anticipation. I picked it up several times only to put it back down. Finally, closing my eyes, I picked the sandwich up again and ate it quickly, in several big bites. All day I sat around nervously, waiting for something to happen. Nothing happened.

I went to school the next day. I don't remember what transpired, but whatever it was I seem to have survived it, and now sable is one of my favorite foods.

# MRS. ZABELL'S WRIST

My first erotic experience, as far as I can remember, was the one involving Mrs. Zabell's wrist. Mrs. Zabell was the lady at the local pharmacy. It was Mother's Day, and I was ten years old. I had decided to buy my mother a bottle of cologne, Arpège. I knew about Arpège from the commercials: "Promise her anything, but give her Arpège." So I went to the corner pharmacy and asked Mrs. Zabell for a bottle of Arpège, but she threw me a curveball. "I have some other fragrances that are very nice and less expensive," she said.

"That's all right," I said, sticking to my guns, "I'll take Arpège."

"Why don't you see if you like one of the others," she persisted, and dabbed some cologne on her wrist. She inched her wrist toward my face. I started turning red. "Go ahead, sniff," she gently ordered.

"That's okay," I said, nervously, "I'll take Arpège."

"Don't be shy," she said. "It won't hurt to try."

I was horrified and excited at the same time. And I sniffed. But I couldn't make any sense of the smell because I was so confused. "It's very nice," I said, my

voice quavering, "but I'd still like the Arpège." And Mrs.
Zabell, her initiation finished, backed down and sold me
what I had come for.

# PORN

When I was a kid I discovered a copy of *Fanny Hill* in our apartment. It was a yellowing paperback and it featured an introduction that discussed the book's literary merits. I myself don't feel qualified to argue *Fanny Hill's* literary merits because all I can remember of the text are references to dildos (I had no idea what they were, but I found the word fascinating) and spankings (always with brushes). I think I remember these things from *Fanny Hill*, though I might have seen them in any of the other pornography the kids on my block often got their hands on. There was one kid in particular (he shall remain nameless), a couple of years my senior, who always seemed to have some form of pornography, either literary or visual. I remember I was once looking at one of this kid's magazines with my friend Michael. I was about eleven at the time. The magazine was open to the centerfold, and Michael said, in a perplexed tone of voice, "My dick gets hard when I look at this." To which the older and wiser aficionado replied, authoritatively, "That's good—that's supposed to happen."

# WHOERS

Brooklyn kids always pronounced the common word for a prostitute as two syllables: who-er. I had no idea how it was spelled, having never seen the word in print before my teens, as far as I can remember, but I assumed it was either whoer or hooer.

If you wanted to insult another kid you'd say, "Your mother's a whoer."

There was a transient hotel in the old neighborhood, the Hotel Oak. Everybody said it was a whoer house

Some of the older guys in the neighborhood would talk about going to Pacific Street (in now-gentrified Boerum Hill) to pick up whoers. I have no idea where they went once they picked them up, but I do know that several of them picked up the clap.

There was a knock-knock joke that went around P.S. 217 that depended on the two-syllable pronunciation. A boy would say to a girl, "Knock-a knock-a." If the girl replied, "Who's there?" the boy would say, "No, you have to do it with an Italian accent: who's-a there-a." So the girl would say, "OK, who's-a there-a?" And the boy would say, "Me-a." And the girl would say, "Me-a who-a?" And the boy would laugh and point at the girl and say, "Ha ha, you're a whoer!"

When I finally saw the word "whore" in print I was confused. I was able to figure out from the context that it was the same word, but it seemed like a strange way to spell whoer. I wondered if it was a typo.

Since I left the old neighborhood, in 1978, first for Park Slope, then the East Village, then back to Park Slope, a snob-appeal neighborhood that's nothing like the Brooklyn of my youth, I've hardly ever heard the two-syllable pronunciation of whore. But recently, as I was walking in Bay Ridge, on my way to lunch at a Middle Eastern restaurant, I overheard two Brooklyn boys, maybe ten or eleven years old, talking, and one of them said, "Yeah, she's a real whoer." It was strangely comforting.

# I Left My Youth at Fred & Rudy's Candy Store

In Brooklyn, in the sixties, the "candy store" was the local hangout for kids, the crossroads of the neighborhood. Actually, these ubiquitous institutions were a combination of soda fountain, luncheonette and newsstand. This was the kind of place the Shangri Las, three girls from Queens, were talking about when they sang, "I met him at the candy store." We probably called them candy stores because as kids the candy we bought there was the center of our culinary universe. Old New York candy stores had a similar function to the barber shop in small towns and working-class black neighborhoods. They were a place where the generations mixed and local gossip was shared.

There were three candy stores in my immediate neighborhood, but our favorite was Fred and Rudy's. Up front were the newsstand, the candy counter and the ice cream case, where they stored the tubs of Breyer's for our cones. Then, as you moved further into the shop, there was the lunch counter, with revolving stools, of course, and booths. As kids we preferred the counter. It was our bar. We'd sit on stools and drink malteds, or egg creams, or cherry-lime Rickeys, or Rock 'n' Root root beer in frosted mugs, or Cokes, large or small, in official Coke glasses. I remember when the price of a small coke went up from six cents to seven. We often munched on long two-cent stick pretzels while drinking and shooting the bull.

Fred and Rudy were like night and day, good cop and bad cop. Fred Leibowitz was a slight, bald guy with a mustache, a good-humored sweetheart. He reminded me a bit of Groucho Marx. Rudy Schiffman was a big bastard, mean and humorless. We spent less time in the store during Rudy's shifts, especially since he often kicked us out when we got rowdy. There was even a little ditty, well known in the neighborhood, that summed up the two men, sung to the tune of "Camptown Races," but all I can remember now is:

Fred's OK but Rudy stinks,
Doo-dah, doo-dah!

I was a wise guy, even as a little kid, and I was always arousing the ire of Rudy. I remember, when I was eleven or twelve years old I had been learning about largely defunct diseases, a favorite subject of sixth grade social studies in the New York City public schools. Mr. Malachowsky had taught us about scurvy, and rickets, and berri berri, as well as a rare tropical disease called yaws. Well, in Brooklyn we pronounce "yours" and "yaws" the same way. Rudy, when he would take our order, would often say, "What's yours?" So one day I responded, "A rare tropical disease," and my friends on the adjoining stools started cracking up. "Out of the store," Rudy yelled. "All of you!"

When Fred and Rudy weren't looking we'd often stand by the magazine rack and peek at the *Playboy* centerfold. If Rudy caught us he'd make us stop. Fred usually turned a blind eye.

A couple of celebrities grew up in the immediate neighborhood. There was Morty Gunty, whose kids' show I appeared on, but the bigger star was Lainie Kazan, whose real last name was Levine. Lainie, who got her big break as Barbra Streisand's understudy in *Funny Girl*, was extremely well endowed, and in 1970 she did a photo spread for *Playboy*. Lainie was long-gone from the neighborhood by this time, but her mother still lived in the old apartment. Mrs. Levine had to give Fred and Rudy's wide berth for a while after one of the neighborhood wise guys (not me this time) said to her, "Hey Mrs. Levine, I saw your daughter's big tits in *Playboy*—Hubba-hubba!"

Fred and Rudy's closed some time in the seventies, a few years before I left the old neighborhood. I always think of Fred and Rudy's whenever I hear "Leader of the Pack," but, unlike that girl from the Shangri-Las, I never met my true love at the candy store. I did, however, sneak a peek at Lainie's tits in *Playboy*—when Fred was minding the store, of course.

# CHINESE FOOD, THE EARLY YEARS

Growing up Jewish in Brooklyn, Chinese food is a birthright, and I was weaned on chicken chow mein, the quintessential Chinese-American dish of my youth. Of course, chow mein as it was served in the Americanized Cantonese restaurants of yore bore little relation to true chow mein, freshly pan-fried wheat noodles. Somewhere along the line, I guess in the U.S., the dry, crispy noodle, or chow mein noodle (which I guess translates as "fried noodle noodle") was invented, and this replaced freshly fried noodles in chow mein. So the chow mein of my youth was basically chicken, or some other meat, with vegetables (mostly celery, if I remember correctly), in a mucus-like sauce that made prodigious use of cornstarch, with dry, crispy noodles thrown on top.

Most of my early Chinese restaurant experiences took place at two restaurants in Midwood. One of them was New Toy Sun, which was across the street from my grammar school, P.S. 217. When I was a kid I loved the idea of a restaurant named after a toy sun. However, it was really an Americanization of Toisan (Taishan in Pinyin), an area of Guangdong province that many early Chinese immigrants came from. It was your basic "one from column A, one from column B" type of place. Spare ribs, egg rolls and fried rice usually figured in a meal. On a splurge we might get shrimp with lobster sauce, which was shrimp in a mucus and egg sauce. Occasionally somebody would go wild and order something "exotic," like wor shew opp (fried pressed duck). This was the kind of Chinese food that had been served in North America for over fifty years, almost exclusively. Restaurants of this ilk were sometimes referred to as "chop suey joints," after that other ubiquitous Chinese-American dish that, except for the absence of noodles, was pretty similar to chow mein. These restaurants always had a section called "American Dishes," usually at the lower right-hand corner of the menu, including things like sandwiches, steak and roast chicken. I never saw anybody order from that section.

The restaurant we mostly patronized was Joy Fong, on Avenue J, a now-defunct place that retains an almost holy status in the memories of Brooklyn Jews of a certain age. I wouldn't be surprised if people visit the site of the former restaurant and wail against the wall. All issues of authenticity aside, I too retain some fond Joy Fong memories. Their spare ribs were meaty and delicious, among the best Chinese-style ribs I've had to this day. The place was extremely popular, and I believe Sunday was the biggest family night out, when you could go deaf from the clatter of competing yentas.

Of course, there was also the occasional trip to Chinatown. Back in the '60s little Cantonese rice shops, like Hong Fat, Lin's Garden and Wo Hop dominated the

Chinatown landscape. Their fare was more authentically Chinese, but much of it was heavy and greasy, quite different from the more upscale Hong Kong seafood places that would arrive somewhat later. It was at restaurants like this that I became familiar with chow fun, which was never available at the Chinese-American neighborhood joints.

Things changed drastically in the early-70s, when regional Chinese cuisines other than Cantonese arrived in New York (and California), eventually transforming the menus at Chinese restaurants all over America.

For years, shunning the "inauthentic," I avoided Chinese restaurants that served the bland, Americanized food of my youth. Now I see it as part of America's culinary heritage and seek out the few places that still serve it.

# My Life of Crime

I learned about organizational structure at a tender age. When I was about ten years old I was part of a shoplifting ring in my neighborhood. Many of the kids had been shoplifting from the local candy stores and supermarkets, and at some point a bunch of us decided to band together, to combine forces. Some of the kids felt we needed a ringleader, but others, myself included, felt that it should be all for one and one for all. The ringleader contingent had the numbers, but when it came time for a vote nobody could agree on a leader. It was decided that a ringleader would be recruited from without, and that the candidate must have particularly strong credentials. To many of the kids that meant only one person—the notorious Butchie Cohen, Jewish thug. Butchie was fourteen and his résumé was impressive: he had beaten up numerous kids, talked back to grownups for years, killed the pets of several of his enemies, and stolen more than the rest of us put together. I neither liked nor trusted Butchie and I felt that to make him ringleader would be a dangerous move, but apparently many of the others believed there was indeed honor among thieves.

Well, Butchie certainly got us organized. No longer

would there be haphazard shoplifting, now we'd have teams, and shifts. Butchie called the shots. He told us what to steal, and how much of it. He gave us pointers on technique. Two or three kids would go into Janoff's candy store, or Fred and Rudy's, and while one kid acted as a decoy, occupying the attention of the man behind the counter, the others would carefully slide packs of gum, boxes of Jujubes and Dots and Junior Mints into their pockets. We had several large boxes, hidden in the basement of one the apartment buildings on Avenue H, to store the candy in. The idea, so Butchie told us, was that we'd collect the stuff for a month or two, and then it would be doled out equally. That way, he said, it would be really special when we finally split up the booty—we could have a party. It sounded like a good idea, but several days before the candy was to be divvied up, a couple of the kids went to the basement to deposit their take for the day and discovered that the boxes were missing. They called a meeting, rank and file, without Butchie. We all agreed that Butchie and only Butchie could be responsible for such a dastardly deed, but when we confronted him he played dumb, said the boxes must have been stolen by some Catholic kids who had gotten wind of our shoplifting ring.

I learned that Butchie died rather young, in his forties, of a heart attack likely resulting from years of drug abuse and a profligate lifestyle. As for the rest of the kids in the ring, some are doctors, some lawyers, others salesmen and small businessmen, and I'm writing this.

# THE BEST BAR MITZVAH

The best bar mitzvah I ever attended, though I didn't realize it at the time, was that of Howard P. Howard wasn't even a friend of mine, just a casual acquaintance from the extended neighborhood who went to the same schools. But he was a good friend of my good friend Michael Z. To my surprise he invited me to his bar mitzvah.

Howard was a lot less well off than most of my friends. His parents were Polish immigrants, and I believe his father was a barber. Instead of hiring a catering hall, the reception was held in their apartment, a casual gathering. I remember standing in the apartment crowded with guests, eating cold cuts, the food for the party. I remember Howard's father shaking my hand and thanking me for coming. This was the only bar mitzvah party of its kind I ever attended. All the rest were at glitzy catering halls where the main dinner course was always prime ribs of beef au jus (a joke among us kids was "Or jus' what?"). Howard's party was a simple celebration while all the others were status symbols. Its humility and inclusiveness touches me these many years later.

The amazing thing is that I remember the party fairly

vividly, when the only other bar mitzvah I have any memories of is my own. I also remember Howard's complicated four-syllable Polish family name, which we pronounced "Puskaluskey," but was spelled differently.

# THE WORST THANKSGIVING

My worst Thanksgiving was the one where I ate a Swanson turkey TV dinner, alone. I think I was about nineteen at the time, and in the midst of a brief depression.

My brief depression lasted about fifteen years, roughly from the ages of eight to twenty-three. I was a miserable kid, adolescent, teenager and young adult. My moods ranged from unhappy to inconsolable despair. I made several (probably half-assed) suicide attempts as a teen, one of them in 1970, after attending the first Earth Day festivities at Union Square. Now Earth Days fill me with relief mixed with a twinge of nostalgic misery.

From a bright, outgoing, skinny kid I turned into a chubby recluse. I started gaining weight during a hellish summer at sleep-away camp, when I was eight. By around eleven or twelve I was pretty much a hermit, keeping to my room, refusing entreaties to come out and play. I wanted to be invisible. I used to walk down the street staring at my shoes. By junior high I made a new set of "friends" and discovered pot and alcohol (and antiwar demonstrations). LSD was reserved for special occasions, like concerts at the Fillmore East or all-night Marx Brothers marathons at the Elgin Theater, on

Eighth Avenue. There was a crowd I hung out with, till all hours, but I wouldn't say that more than a few were real friends, though I remember some of them quite fondly—brilliant, funny kids, all troubled in different ways.

Things got a little better when I got to college and started discovering my voice as a writer. But my psyche was still fragile. I think I may have turned down a Thanksgiving invitation when I was nineteen and chose to "celebrate" alone with my Swanson TV dinner.

The real turning point in my life came when I moved to the East Village, in 1979. For a Brooklyn kid, finally getting to Manhattan was a triumph. I felt I finally had control of my life. And I was fortunate to dive headlong into one of the most vibrant literary and performance scenes New York City has ever known.

I don't think I've ever been really, truly miserable since. I joke that I've had more than my quota of misery. Even when I was unemployed for the greater part of a four-year period, not so long ago, I didn't despair. People would ask if I was depressed. "Not really," I'd say. "I'm anxious all the time and unhappy some of the time, but I'm also happy most of the time, at the same time. I'm emotionally multitasking."

You can't second-guess or judge anybody's misery. You can't tell a depressed teenager that they have everything, or that they're being selfish, or that things will get better (even if they usually do). Their despair is real, I know. If I could tell a teenager on the brink of suicide anything it would be: hang in there, I know it's unbearable, but there'll come a time when you can call the shots, when you can tell all the people who are fucking you over to go fuck themselves, or ignore them, it'll be your choice.

# THIS TOO SHALL PASS

I don't do my own laundry, I send mine out to a place that does wash, dry and fold. I picked up a bag that I had dropped off earlier in the day. I took the clothes out of the bag, ready to put the pieces in various drawers and closets, when I came across an item that I was sure didn't belong to me. It was a T-shirt I had never seen before, yet it had my photo silkscreened on it, an old photo, from the '70s, I think, though I can't remember ever having seen this photo before. I was wearing a shirt with a long, pointy collar and oversize glasses frames. I looked at my own face from those many years ago. I looked very sad. Very sad. Under my image were the words, "This Too Shall Pass."

# PART II

# THE ENERGY

I was eating solo at a local Middle Eastern restaurant, a favorite of mine. At one point, when I was maybe 2/3 through my falafel platter, as I was dipping my pita into the hummus, a woman at a nearby table turned to me and said, "Excuse me, sir, I don't mean to interrupt you, but you seem to really be enjoying yourself. I just had to tell you that."

I was taken aback. "Well, the food is very good here, right?" I answered after a moment's pause.

"It's not just the food," she said. "I mean you really seem to be enjoying yourself. I can feel the energy from here." Her companion nodded in assent.

This was news to me. I had no idea I had any energy. To tell the truth, I had been having a pretty mediocre, if not miserable, day. In fact, I was feeling a bit depressed. Now, out of the blue, a stranger is telling me that I'm very obviously enjoying myself—and projecting energy, no less. So maybe I wasn't depressed after all. All of a sudden I was feeling great.

Sometimes a stranger is as good as a friend.

# CLEANING WOMAN

Since I do my writing at home, I decided to hire a cleaning woman, in the hope that a cleaner, more orderly space would be helpful to my work, as well as to my general well-being.

When the cleaning woman arrived, I told her I was taking my laptop to a coffee shop to do some writing while she cleaned the apartment. As I was about to leave I noticed the cleaning woman had changed into her work clothes. I told her I'd return in four hours.

A few minutes before the agreed-upon time, I started walking home, looking forward to my spiffy clean work and living space. I unlocked the door, entered the apartment, and was shocked. The apartment was not what I would call clean and orderly at all. All my possessions, my clothes, sheets, dishes, supplies, etc., had been removed from their closets, their drawers, their cupboards, and were stacked in piles around the apartment, leaving little room to move around. All my books had been taken down from their cases, likewise my CDs. I also noticed that the cleaning woman had changed back into her civvies.

"What on earth is going on?" I asked, both

flabbergasted and exasperated.

"It is to purify," the cleaning woman replied, in the characteristic accent of her countrywomen, as she left the apartment.

# BECOMING PETE

I became Pete in 1981, when I grew a beard and started wearing contact lenses. Or was it about a year later, when I shaved the beard and started wearing the black horn-rimmed glasses that would define my face for years to come? I am sure the change from Peter to Pete as my *nom de monde*, as I call it, to distinguish it from my *nom de plume*, went part and parcel with a change in facial appearance.

What was going on in the early-80s? Well, I was in my mid-twenties, and just settling into an adult sense of self, and I guess I was trying out different modes of self-presentation.

The beard didn't work for me. Besides giving me an ongoing facial itch, when it grew bushy with flecks of red it gave me the mien of a terrorist, which I guess was not a look I wanted to cultivate. And I could never get accustomed to contacts. My eyes were always dry, and I couldn't really get used to my face without glasses after wearing them for over a decade. There's something to be said for high cheekbones and deep-set eyes, sure, but I felt that glasses mitigated what I considered to be a mildly Neanderthal appearance (especially pronounced in my brief beard period).

I was coming to a sense of adult self both as a person and as a writer, and I think I wanted to create two intersecting personae, Pete the person and Peter the writer. That part, actually, wasn't new. My earliest publications bore my middle initial, N, which I had never used in other contexts. I think that was because even as a teenager I wanted to separate my writer self from my everyday self. I think the change to Pete came shortly after I dropped the middle initial from my *nom de plume*. Or maybe at the same time.

And perhaps I also felt that the more informal Pete would, however subtly, make me more comfortably feel part of collegial, congenial society, something I had felt apart from during the long depression that lasted from adolescence to my early twenties. Funny, I hadn't thought about that before.

Peter. The writer, the man obsessed with crafting sentences, and with a certain kind of order.

Pete. Regular guy. All-American guy. The kind of guy you could toss back a couple of brewskies with and laugh together at the follies of the universe, at the chaos.

All right, that's probably pushing it.

# THE NIGHT I MISSED
# THANKSGIVING

One November night some years ago, I was walking to Chinatown for Thanksgiving dinner (a long-standing tradition among my friends who don't have family in New York). When I got to where the restaurant was supposed to be, I saw a church that looked like one of those 17th-century Portuguese colonial churches I'd seen in various parts of Asia. There was a sign hanging on the outside of the church that said Canton City, but I figured the restaurant wasn't in the main part of the church. I couldn't find the entrance to the restaurant, so I walked up the stairs to the main church entrance. A Chinese teenager carrying a skateboard was coming out through the big wooden door and he held it for me. Inside, the nave was painted pastel blue and white. It reminded me of a church I had seen in Macau. I went back out and kept looking for the restaurant. Finally I saw a glass door around the corner, at the side of the church building. I walked in and found myself in a big, glitzy restaurant.

My friends were all already at a large round table. It turned out that I was very late. My friends were all hungry. I was going to do the ordering, and I had pretty much planned out the meal by studying the menu in advance. Much to my surprise and horror, however, the menu was completely different than the one I had studied. No dish was the same. In fact, I was unfamiliar with all the dishes, though many sounded interesting. That was part of the problem, actually. Too many of them sounded interesting, and I had to order a nicely balanced meal for eight. I kept studying the menu, and I couldn't decide what to order. I was filled with anxiety. I could see that my friends were getting hungry. Then I noticed that Fan, a waiter I knew from two defunct restaurants I used to frequent, was working there. That's good, I thought, he can help me with the menu. But he wasn't coming by our table, and I couldn't get any of the staff's attention. I also noticed at this time that there was a basket full of western-style dinner rolls on the table. A friend was reaching for one. "Don't eat it," I said. "You'll ruin your appetite." He looked disappointed (and hungry). Finally after about an hour of perusing the menu I decided what to order. But I couldn't get the attention of any of the wait staff. I decided to go in search of Fan.

I walked into another room that turned out to be a bar filled with hard-drinking Chinese men smoking cigarettes. I thought I heard Fan's voice, but I couldn't find him. I walked into another room that turned out to be a Chinese bakery. All the clientele and staff were women and they looked at me oddly, like I didn't belong there. I left the bakery. Back on the street, I went back to the side of the church where the entrance had been, but I couldn't find it. I walked a bit and went into a nearby shop to see if anybody could help me. The proprietors, a man and a woman, looked Goan (there's a particular mix of Portuguese and Indian features I can recognize). I asked them if they had any idea where the entrance to Canton City was. The man and the woman spoke to each other in a language I couldn't understand. Then the man said to me, "That's in the Portuguese church, right?"

"I suppose it's Portuguese," I said.

He gave me directions to the church, but didn't say anything about how I'd get into the restaurant. It also turned out that the shop was further away from the church than I had thought, about three blocks. I walked in the direction of the church, and I saw a beautiful crepuscular light, giving the church a mysterious and majestic look. This is wonderful, I thought to myself, to see something like this in New York makes up for all my troubles. But my pleasure was short-lived. When I got back to the church I still couldn't find the entrance to Canton City. I did see a Chinese bakery, though. I figured I could enter through the bakery and find my way back into the restaurant. But this was a different bakery with no passageway. I felt terrible about holding up my friends' dinner. Frustrated, I went home, hoping my friends had gone ahead and ordered.

When I got back to my apartment, I turned on the TV. A woman who was hopelessly late for a meeting with her girlfriend had brought an award to present to the friend, the "Patient, Loyal Friend Award." This show is a parable for my situation, I thought. The woman was anxious as to whether the friend would accept the award, and I empathized. Then the announcer said, "After this commercial break, find out whether the friend accepts the award or kicks her out." I was on the edge of my seat. After the commercial the woman presented the award to her friend. The friend disdainfully handed it back to her and said, "Enjoy your friendship."

# OLGA'S PARTY

It must have been about 1981 or '82. I had been invited to a party at Olga's, in Soho. Olga used to throw these very artsy parties on a regular basis. This one was a cocktail party at eight, and I had a little time to kill, so I stopped by a bar in the West Village.

I was sitting at the bar, sipping a Stoli, when this guy tapped me on the shoulder. I looked up. "Peter Cherches?"

"Yes," I said.

"You don't remember me, do you?"

"Well, to be quite honest, I don't."

"Rocco Cataldo, eighth grade social studies! Mrs. Harris."

"Rocco," I said, "it's been a long time!"

"Yeah, it has. But I've been hearing a lot about you lately. I hear you're a great writer. I can't say I've read anything you've written, but I've been hearing a lot of wonderful things."

"Well, that's really nice to hear."

"Yeah, and speaking of writing, I've got a little favor to

ask of you."

"Oh?" I asked suspiciously.

"Well, remember that term paper we had to do for Mrs. Harris's class?"

"Yeah."

"Well, I was doing a report on Ponce de Leon's search for the fountain of youth and, well, I don't know how to ask this, but it would be a great help if you could look over the paper and correct the grammar. You are a writer, after all."

"But Rocco," I said, "that was years ago."

"Yeah, I know," he said. "I guess I've had some kind of block or something. But I'd really like to get out of eighth grade, so do you think you could help me?"

"Well, I'm pretty busy."

"But you gotta do it, for old time's sake. It'll only take a couple of minutes."

I just wanted to get this guy off my back, so I said, "All right, Rocco, I'll tell you what. I've got to leave now to go to a party, but I come here pretty often, so why don't you meet me here same time next Friday and we can go over the paper."

"Gee, thanks Peter. I always knew you were a great guy."

"You can call me Pete," I said, and I left the bar.

I walked down to Spring Street. When I got to Olga's

loft I saw the usual crowd. Not necessarily the same people, but the usual crowd. I started mingling and then Olga approached me. "Pete, I'm very glad you could make it," she said. "You must come look at the art. I've arranged a conceptual installation for this party and I'm very excited."

I followed Olga to a corner of the room. There, suspended from the ceiling, hanging by a rope tied around her ankles, was a naked woman. A crowd of people stood around, staring. Olga was called away and I stayed to admire the art. After a while, the naked woman spoke to me. "Aren't you Peter Cherches?"

"Yes," I said, startled.

"You don't remember me, do you?" she asked.

"Well, to be quite honest, I don't. Maybe it's the position, but you don't look familiar."

"Susan Lieberman, eighth grade social studies."

This is very strange, I thought.

"I've been hearing a lot about your writing, Peter," she said.

"Please, call me Pete."

"OK, Pete. I can't say I've read anything of yours yet, but I've been hearing an awful lot of wonderful things."

"Well, that's nice to hear," I said. "And what have you been up to—just hanging around?"

"Actually, I'm a painter," she said.

"Oh?"

"Yes, I'm a New Expressionist."

"So what are you doing here?" I asked.

"Oh, I'm just doing this for the money. I work for an agency that hires starving artists out as conceptual art."

Just then Olga returned and said, "Pete, you must come with me. There's a gentleman who wants to say hello." She took me to where a very tall man was standing.

"Hello Pete," the man said. He must have seen that I didn't recognize him, because he said, "You don't recognize me, do you?"

"Well, to be quite honest, I don't," I said.

"Bart Randall. We met at Olga's last party."

"Oh, right. You're an actor, aren't you?"

"Yes, and you're a writer. I do remember. And ever since we've met I've been hearing all sorts of wonderful things about your writing. Can't say I've read anything, though. But tell me, Pete, have you seen Jack Billingsly's production of Streetcar at La Mama?"

"Why yes, as a matter of fact, I have."

"Tell me honestly—what did you think of my performance?"

"Oh, were you in it?"

"Yes I was."

"Who did you play?"

"Blanche."

"Blanche?" I asked incredulously.

"Yes, I played Blanche DuBois. What did you think of my performance?"

I had to think for a minute. Finally, I said, "Well, it's clear to me that you're either a great actor or a very good female impersonator."

"The former, I should hope," he said.

Just then I heard a loud thud. The rope that had been holding up Susan Lieberman had broken and she came crashing down to the floor. Everybody was running over to make sure she was all right. I saw the diversion as my opportunity to make my getaway, and I left the party.

# DOWNTOWN MADE ME

Back in the eighties I was a "downtown writer," by virtue of residence and associations as much as, if not more than, style.

Downtown Manhattan has always been a hotbed of bohemianism and experimentation. By the time of my downtown, however, once-bohemian Greenwich Village no longer had any real significance in the equation. I'd say that the downtown scene I worked within was born largely of the convergence of the sixties East Village counter-culture and the genre-crossing Soho scene of the seventies (even if that was really just a heating up of things that had started brewing in the sixties). While collaborations among artists, writers and musicians had a long history in New York, in my downtown the distinctions between who was what had blurred. My downtown was a stew.

I moved to the East Village from Brooklyn in 1979. I had found the perfect apartment to be a downtown writer in. It was a dark, gloomy first-floor tenement apartment on East 10th Street, just west of Tompkins Square Park, on the block with the Russian Baths, a Ukrainian Church, and the Boys Club, not to mention Carlo Pittore's Galleria dell'Occhio, the mail artist's window gallery. My apartment had a bathtub in the kitchen, a tiny water closet, crumbling walls and a ceiling that once ended up on my floor. At least I had my own toilet. Some buildings still had shared toilets down the hall.

By this time I had been publishing my work in literary magazines for a couple of years and was also editor of my own magazine, *Zone*. I had moved to the East Village because all sorts of interesting things were happening there, and at age 23 I needed to be in the thick of it. Over the next eight years, which I'll nostalgically declare the chronological heart of the downtown scene, things got out of control in all the best ways. New magazines and performance venues seemed to be launched every week. Writers and painters formed rock bands. Painters made performance pieces, writers made performance pieces, writers, painters and musicians collaborated on performance pieces. I started performing.

My performance career was not really anything I had planned. It grew out of what was supposed to be a reading at The Performing Garage. I had met Liz LeCompte, Spalding Gray and The Wooster Group when I had documented their theater piece "Point Judith" for *Zone*. I think it must have been 1980 when they decided to do a reading series in the space and invited me to appear. I always loved doing readings, connecting with a live audience, and I had also become really interested in much of the text-based performance work that was happening at the time. Something clicked. Performing

Garage, I thought; I can't just sit there and read from the page. So I turned my texts into performance pieces. It worked, I was hooked, and for the rest of the decade I was a performer as well as a writer.

Some of the performance work I did was solo, but much was in collaboration with musicians. In 1981 I was introduced to the improvising multi-instrumentalist Elliott Sharp by a mutual friend. I was interested in working with music in my performance and Elliott was interested in working with text. We got together, worked up a bunch of pieces based on some of my texts, decided we were onto something and called it Sonorexia, because we wanted a name that sounded like a disease. Except it wasn't a disease. The neologism means appetite for sound.

Sonorexia performed regularly at many of the major East Village and Soho performance venues of the time, like 8BC, Darinka and Inroads, but we also did one-shots at the Mudd Club (on a bill with poet Bob Holman as "Panic DJ") and CBGB (where Richard Hell slept on a table during our show). Gary Ray Bugarcic's Darinka, on East 1st Street, was like a second home to me. I did countless performances there and also curated a monthly fiction reading series. Darinka doesn't get the recognition it deserves in histories of the scene.

During that time I was working nights as a legal proofreader, a job that attracted many writers, dancers and actors. One of my favorite coworkers, Jim Moisan, was the creator of the comic book hero "Bill Dupp, Soho

Detective." Keyboardist and songwriter Lee Feldman was another proofreader, and we became close collaborators, writing songs together as well as performing monologues with live soundtracks that we called "Movies for the Ears."

During the day, those days, you could stumble into any of a number of East Village eateries and join a table of writers or musicians to ruminate on life and art and more mundane matters over a cup of Joe. Of course, when you're in your twenties hanging out is a major occupation. A place called White Wave on Second Avenue was a favorite late breakfast spot of downtown musicians who straddled the genres of free improv, no wave and jazz. The more jazz-oriented of the bunch, like Phillip Johnston, Joel Forrester and Wayne Horvitz later worked with me on my Thelonious Monk project. From breakfast I usually went straight to a lunch engagement, then back home to do a little writing, then to my job, then to an after-midnight dinner at places like Baltyk, a Polish restaurant with a killer white borscht, or perhaps 103 Second Avenue. Then I'd go home, watch the news with Linda Ellerbee, get a little sleep, and roll back out to breakfast and the invigorating sustenance of chat.

I think the most prominent view of downtown writing of those years is that it was dominated by raw, gritty work that was heavy on sex and violence of all flavors. Indeed, many of my peers fit into a gestalt that was heavily inspired by Genet, Burroughs, Hubert Selby, Henry Miller, and of course Rimbaud. But some of us were more interested in the prose piece (or more elementally the sentence) as object, mining territory that was much more informed by European avant-garde traditions, Gertrude Stein, and older or near-contemporary American writers like Harry Mathews, Russell Edson and Walter Abish. Writers like Holly Anderson, Roberta Allen and the wacky dada minimalist Mike Topp are among those I feel a literary affinity with, but the great thing about that period was that regardless of approach we were, for the most part, a big extended family, often sharing readings at places like ABC No Rio and more often the pages of magazines like *Between C & D* and *Redtape*.

I mention those two magazines not only because they were the most quintessentially East Village or Alphabet City of the bunch, but also because they nurtured that kind of extended family mode I'm talking about. I don't think it would be hyperbole to call *Between C & D* a legendary magazine. It was the baby of writers Joel Rose and Catherine Texier, and was published out of their apartment on 7th street, between, you guessed it, C & D. The magazine played ironically upon the Alphabet City location with a drug culture meets technology design aesthetic. The magazine was printed on fanfold paper on Epson dot-matrix printers, and slipped into ziploc bags. They had a bunch of these printers in the apartment, donated by Epson after someone at the company had read about the magazine. The din of printers churning out copies was the soundtrack to Joel & Catherine's life. The great thing about the two of them, and the magazine, was the trust and respect they had for their writers. A number of us were regulars, appearing in multiple issues, and lots of different styles and approaches were represented. Among this crew were Patrick McGrath, whose work in *Between C & D* paved the way for his very successful later career, Dennis Cooper, Lynne Tillman, and Darius James, arguably the most significant African-American voice in downtown writing of that era. With *Between C & D* it was rarely an issue of waiting for acceptance or rejection, it was just an issue of which issue your piece was going to be in. For certain of us, at least, Joel and Catherine had implicit trust. If we thought a piece of ours was good enough for them to publish that was good enough for them. Michael Carter of *Redtape* worked in much the same way, if on a more erratic schedule. What a luxury that was for a writer.

A looming figure of the downtown literary scene those days, the booster par excellence, was poet and bookstore guy Ron Kolm. I first met Ron when people started telling me about a guy at a Soho bookstore who would buttonhole customers and insist that they buy my chapbook *Bagatelles*. Ron was responsible for my appearance in a number of magazines and anthologies, some of which he published himself and some for which he acted as a sort of agent without portfolio. Ron is a pack rat and his extensive archive formed the nucleus of the Downtown Collection at NYU's Fales Library.

My other significant publishing associations of

the time included those with *Benzene* magazine and Purgatory Pie Press. I had met Allan Bealy and Sheila Keenan of *Benzene* in 1980, just before they published their first issue. It was at a party I threw with my *Zone* co-editor Dennis DeForge at a Bowery loft where we had hoped to open a gallery and performance space. The Zone Gallery never happened, but a fruitful association and lasting friendships grew out of that party. My work appeared regularly in *Benzene*, and the press published my short prose collection *Condensed Book* in 1986. *Benzene* had a more Soho/Tribeca aesthetic than an East Village one. Its multimedia focus was served well by its large tabloid format. It was one of the major publications documenting the era, and it had an important influence on the later direction of *Zone* magazine. Dikko Faust and Esther K. Smith of Purgatory Pie Press are the edgiest letterpress printer/publishers I know, and they've done three books of mine, two of them hybrid verbo-visual works, all out of print.

I lived in the East Village from 1979 to 1987. This was my most productive period as a writer, but I was, after all, in my twenties. Without a doubt the work I produced was greatly influenced by the hothouse nature of that time and place. Graham Greene wrote a novel titled *England Made Me*. Well, downtown made me. The East Village went through a lot of changes in those years. When I first moved to 10th Street there were abandoned buildings used by junkies as shooting galleries. A few years later Patti Astor's Fun Gallery had opened on the block, but the East Village art gallery scene was a short-lived phenomenon. By the time I left in '87 real estate prices had skyrocketed. I used to say that when I moved into the neighborhood people came in limos to buy dope, then they came in limos to buy art, and finally they came in limos to buy apartments. The Tomkins Square riots happened the year after I left, and for me that conveniently marks the end of an era. But maybe that's just because I was gone.

Since then I've been living back in Brooklyn, but for me those years were a dream confluence of age, scene and time. To be a writer in one's twenties, in the East Village, in the eighties: now that was really something.

# THE KNISH

I had picked up a knish at the deli, a potato knish. You could say I'm a knish lover. I love all kinds of knishes, but potato is my favorite, especially the baked ones—the round ones. The square ones, which are fried, are OK too, but I prefer the baked ones, especially with mustard. I had the deli man put mustard on my knish before he wrapped it for me. My mouth was watering. I couldn't wait to eat my round, baked potato knish with mustard. When I got back to the apartment I sat down at the table in my living room and unwrapped the knish. It was beautiful. I picked it up, brought it to my mouth, opened my mouth, and was about to take a bite when I heard a crash. What was that? I put the knish down and ran into the kitchen, where the sound seemed to be coming from. Damn—it was the ceiling. A big section of ceiling had fallen, from where there had been a leak a week earlier. Now my floor was full of dust and chunks of ceiling. My priorities were: sweep up and call the landlord. The knish would have to wait. So I swept the floor and bagged the debris. Afterwards I called the landlord. I got his machine and left a message. Then, finally, I returned to my knish. It was cold. I should have expected that. Cold knishes are not very appetizing. But

I did have my heart set on that knish. Cold or not, I was going to eat it. So I picked it up, brought it to my mouth, opened my mouth, and heard a knock at my door. I put the knish down and went to answer the door. It was Harold, my next-door neighbor.

"I heard a crash," he said. "Is everything all right?"

I told him about the ceiling, and that I had left a message for the landlord, and he went back to his apartment.

I returned to my knish. It was ice-cold. The mustard was drying out, getting crusty. The thing was not in the least bit appetizing now. But I wanted it! I couldn't help it. Appetizing or not, I wanted that knish. So I picked it up, brought it to my mouth, opened my mouth—and the phone rang. Maybe it's the landlord, I thought. I'd better answer it. So I put the knish down and went to answer the phone. It was indeed the landlord. I told him about the ceiling. He said he'd send a repairman over right away. I knew what right away means coming from a landlord. I wasn't holding my breath.

I got back to the knish. It really looked horrible. The whole thing was drying out. It was starting to smell funny. Really, I should have thrown it out, but I just couldn't do it. In spite of everything, I still wanted it. Even though it was making me sick to think of ingesting it, something compelled me to pick it up, bring it up to my mouth, open my mouth—and then I heard another crash.

I ran into the kitchen. More ceiling. I swept it up and bagged it. No use calling the landlord, I thought, so I returned to the living room. Now the knish was really offensive: hairy mold growing all over it, bugs crawling all over. I sat at the table, staring at it, sick to my stomach from the putrid smell, staring at it for quite some time, then I picked it up, brought it to my mouth, opened my mouth...

# AT DAGWOOD AND BLONDIE'S

Sometime in the mid-eighties I visited Dagwood and Blondie at their home on Long Island. I had told them that I was researching a book on the Sunday funnies, but I was really there for a different reason altogether. I had recently learned that the couple known as Dagwood and Blondie were actually Mr. and Mrs. Hermann Bömstadt, aged ex-Nazis trying to lead quiet, anonymous lives in the suburbs.

Don't jump to conclusions, I told myself. Give them a chance.

I got there without a hitch. They had given me good directions. "Take the first left after you pass the synagogue. We're the third house on the right." Their name was on the mailbox: The Bumsteads. Their lawn was meticulously mowed and greener, it seemed, than any other lawn on the block. Their welcome mat said WELCOME.

I rang the doorbell and Blondie greeted me, saying, "Welcome, Mr. Cherches," surely thinking, "Vilkommen, Herr Cherches." Blondie's real name was Hilda. "Dagwood is not here yet," she told me. "He just left the American Legion. He should be home shortly."

Dagwood, retired for many years, spent most days at the American Legion bar, drinking Beck's beer and eating enormous sandwiches—the kind that are known in Germany as Hermann sandwiches.

While we were waiting for Dagwood, Blondie showed me their collection of Bumstead memorabilia: comic strips, movie stills, and consumer products, like the Dagwood and Blondie bubble bath bottles. When Dagwood got home Blondie served dinner, an American classic, franks and beans. We drank Budweiser. During dinner the Bumsteads reminisced, for my benefit. Dagwood told me several funny Mr. Dithers stories. I found them both quite charming, but at one point in the conversation Dagwood made a telling slip. "Good knockwurst, yes?" he asked, immediately turning red. There was a nervous silence and then Blondie changed the subject.

After dinner we sat around for a while, just talking. They did their best to make me feel welcome, made sure my beer mug was always full. Then Dagwood turned on the television. "Our favorite show," he said. "Please. I hope you don't mind."

"Not at all," I said, and I moved to the sofa. I sat there, between the Bumsteads, munching on pretzels, drinking beer, watching Letterman, laughing at the jokes of a Jewish comedian as we jovially elbowed each other, knowing I'd have to file my report the following day.

# CUTTING THE CABLE

I recently got rid of my cable and bought a digital antenna. I set it up and started scanning for stations. I was most concerned that channel 13, PBS, would come in clearly. Great—it was clear as a bell, in HD, no different from what I was getting from cable, and I was paying them over $30 a month for "basic" service, once the cable box & taxes were figured in. The antenna cost me less than $25.

I started surfing the channels. After passing by a ball game and a couple of sitcoms, I happened upon something that really blew my mind. On the screen were home movies of me as a toddler. WTF? Was this some kind of joke? I stayed glued to the set. After the home movies were over a guy who looked exactly like me came on. I wondered if it were Willie Garson, the actor who played Stanford Blatch on "Sex and the City" and Mozzie on "White Collar." I used to be mistaken for him all the time when he was on "Sex and the City." But the guy's voice was exactly like mine, same timbre, same inflections. He said, "You're watching the Peter Cherches network." Whoever it was, he kept talking about me in the third person. "Next up we have a rare video of Cherches and Elliott Sharp performing 'It's Uncle,'" he continued, "their signature tune as Sonorexia, though the word 'tune' is perhaps a bit of a stretch." And then it came on, a video of me & Sharp doing "It's Uncle" that I never knew existed. It would have been an early Sonorexia performance, ca. 1982, since I still had a beard and contact lenses. I was trying to figure out where this might have been. It wasn't St. Mark's Church or Inroads, two early Sonorexia venues. In fact, it didn't look familiar at all. And then the camera panned back, to the audience. There must have been thousands of people. It was apparently a big sports arena. Sonorexia, our little downtown music-performance act, in an arena!

After that was over I was in for another shock. It was footage of the play I was in at Camp Skymount in 1963, when I was seven. I played the Mayor of Hamelin in "The Pied Piper." I had done great in all the rehearsals, but on the night of the performance I flubbed all of my lines. I was like Ralph Kramden, going "Hum-a-na-hum-a-na." The prompter had to feed me all my lines. It was a great embarrassment. So I watched the film of the play with trepidation, but, much to my surprise, in this film I got all my lines right.

Of course I set the station as one of my favorites.

# An Uncanny Resemblance

Geri and I had just finished lunch at the Bagel Nosh. We were heading back to her office at *Sport* magazine, where she was art director, and where I sometimes picked up freelance proofreading work, when we were approached by a short, unkempt man in his mid-thirties. "You are Geri Swensen from the *Sport* magazine, yes?" he asked her in a thick German accent.

"Yes," she answered.

"Pigs!" he started screaming. "You people are all pigs!"

I tried to intervene. "Can you please tell us what you're talking about?" I asked.

He went on raving. What I was able to make out was that he was a retired German soccer player. Now that his soccer playing days were over he was unable to find work. He blamed this on the fact that he had never received any coverage in *Sport*. He had come to America to seek his revenge.

I deduced that he was unbalanced, but I tried to reason with him nonetheless. I explained that American sports magazines rarely cover European soccer matches, and that it was nothing personal. He said something about cultural myopia and knocked me down. He grabbed

Geri by the arm and started dragging her down the street. I was dazed; I couldn't get up. "Stop! Kidnap!" I screamed. Nobody paid any attention. I saw the guy drag Geri down the stairs to the subway at the next corner. It was then that I realized that Geri's abductor bore an uncanny resemblance to Rainer Werner Fassbinder, the late German film maker.

I was finally able to get up. Something had to be done, but what? I decided to call Dennis DeForge, my co-editor at *Zone* magazine. I didn't know what he could do, but at least it was someone to talk to while I waited.

Dennis arrived on the scene a few minutes later. I apprised him of the situation. I worked out a strategy: we'd go down into the subway and hide out in one of the tunnels between stops—this guy was bound to show up sooner or later. We found a tunnel that suited our purpose. "What do we do now?" Dennis asked.

"We wait," I said.

So we waited. We waited for hours. Then Dennis said, "Hey, look at that," and pointed down the tunnel. A few hundred feet away from us was a café. I had heard about these cafés before, but I always found it hard to believe that they really existed. Apparently, slumming in subway tunnels had become so popular among New York's gentry that some enterprising restaurateurs had set up a chain of chic cafés right in the tunnels. That gave me an idea.

"They probably have a phone," I said to Dennis. "I'll

go make a call and see if I can get any information." I told Dennis to wait there.

I went to the café. They had a pay phone all right, but it was being used. The guy on the phone seemed to stay on forever. I must have waited at least an hour. I was about to go over and tell him that I had an emergency call to make when he got off. I went over and picked up the receiver. I couldn't get a dial tone. The phone was out of order. Then I noticed that there was another phone. I went over and picked up the receiver. Same thing. No dial tone. It was then that I overheard some people talking about a plane hijacking: "Have you heard the bulletins? A retired German soccer player who bears an uncanny resemblance to Rainer Werner Fassbinder, the late German film maker, has kidnapped the lovely art director of *Sport* magazine and hijacked a plane. He is demanding more coverage of German soccer in the American media."

I ran back to Dennis and told him the news. We couldn't figure out what to do, so we kept waiting in the tunnel. A few hours later, Dennis turned to me and said, "Hey, look over there." He pointed toward the café.

There was Geri, standing at the bar. I ran over and hugged her. "You're safe!" I said elatedly.

"Yes, I'm safe," she said.

There was something frightening about her voice. She spoke in a monotone. It sounded like a recording. Then I noticed that she was carrying copies of *Time* and

*Newsweek*. I had never known Geri to read newsweeklies, so I asked her, "Why do you have those?"

Her answer sounded rehearsed: "Now more than ever, in these times of terrorism and global unrest, I feel it is important to keep abreast of current events."

I was worried, but I chalked her condition up to shock resulting from all she had been through. I asked her about the hijacking. "Where did he take the plane?"

"To the Bowery."

"To the Bowery?" I asked incredulously.

"Yes. He had them land on the Bowery."

I found that rather hard to believe. After all, how do you land a plane on the Bowery? But I went along with it. "So how come it took them so long to find the plane?" I asked.

"Don't be silly," she answered. "You know what a mess it is down there."

# THE FLYER

I was walking down the street, I can't remember where I was headed, when somebody handed me a flyer. Sometimes I take them, sometimes I don't. I took this one, but before I had a chance to look at it a gust of wind came along and blew it out of my hand.

Now odds are that whatever this flyer was announcing would have been of no interest to me, but now, for some reason, I was curious. So I looked around, hoping to find the young woman who had handed me the flyer, but she was nowhere in sight. I was being silly, I know, but I couldn't let it rest. I had to know what was on that flyer.

So I buttonholed strangers on the street. "Excuse me, sir," I'd say, or "Excuse me, madam, have you by any chance seen a flyer flying around?"

"Flyer flying around?" they'd ask, in a tone of voice that suggested we weren't speaking the same language. So I rephrased the question. "By any chance did you just see a circular fly by?" Or, "Did you happen to see a leaflet whiz by?" Still, no luck. I realized I was on my own.

So I began to walk up and down the street, looking for the flyer. I looked under cars and between cars, but no luck. I looked in the doorways of all the buildings. I checked the alleyways between the buildings. I refused to give up, had to find that flyer.

I tried looking down the sewer. Maybe it flew down the sewer. But I couldn't see down the sewer; if the flyer had flown down the sewer it was lost forever. I could not allow myself to believe that.

So I kept looking. I continued to walk up and down the street, looking for the flyer. I picked up every stray piece of paper I saw, but nothing that could be properly called a flyer. I was running out of places to look. Then I saw the garbage can on the corner.

I rummaged through the garbage can, the entire garbage can, through all sorts of disgusting garbage, all sorts of rotting, smelly food; it was all over me and I still hadn't found the flyer. Then I saw another garbage can down the block. I ran to it, as if my life depended on it, and repeated the process. Still no flyer, and I stank like a garbage dump.

I walked, aimlessly, not knowing which direction I was heading, reeking of the city's garbage, utterly dejected by my failure to find the flyer when all of a sudden, from the corner of my eye, I noticed a piece of paper flying through the air. Sailing on the wind. I started chasing after it. It continually receded from my grasp, mocking me. I wanted that piece of paper I wanted that flying piece of paper I wanted that flyer. I chased it for blocks and blocks. At times I came pretty close, but I could never quite catch it. I chased that flyer for miles. Miles and miles. I was out of breath, about to collapse, there was no way I could hold out. And then, miraculously, just in the nick of time, the wind died down and the piece of paper dropped to the ground at the same time I did. I grabbed the flyer. I held on to it for dear life as I caught my breath. After a while I got up, flyer in hand, and began to walk down the street, utterly content, utterly satisfied, utterly relieved that I had finally retrieved that flyer.

And then a thought occurred to me: what if this was not the right flyer after all?

# MR. CHERCHES MAILS A LETTER

It's another day. There are so many of them. Seven days in a week, thirty in a month, or thirty-one, or sometimes twenty-eight or twenty-nine, three hundred sixty-five days in a year, and leap years have an extra day, so many days, so much time to fill, twenty-four hours in a day, sixty minutes an hour, sixty seconds a minute, so much time and so little to do.

It's another day and Mr. Cherches can't decide what to do. What to do, what to do, so much time and so little to do, Mr. Cherches says to himself. What shall I do?

Look out the window, Mr. Cherches.

Mr. Cherches looks out the window. It is a bright, sunny day. What shall I do on this bright, sunny day? Mr. Cherches wonders.

One should go out on a bright, sunny day. Bright, sunny days are just right for going out, just as dark, gloomy days are just right for staying in.

Mr. Cherches stayed in yesterday. Yesterday a dark, gloomy day and Mr. Cherches stayed in. It was a good day for staying in. But Mr. Cherches hates to do the same thing two days in a row, that makes for a boring existence, and anyway, one should not stay in on a bright, sunny day, for bright, sunny days are made for going out.

Go out, Mr. Cherches, go out. It's a bright, sunny day; go out and make the most of it.

But I went out two days ago, Mr. Cherches remembers. And I hate to do the same thing twice in three days, that makes for such a boring existence.

Go out and do something, Mr. Cherches, go out and do something.

Do something! What a delightful idea, Mr. Cherches thinks. Not just go out, but go out and do something, what a marvelous idea. But what to do, what to do, Mr. Cherches wonders. What shall I do on this bright, sunny day?

Take a walk, take a stroll, see the sights, breathe the air.

But I took a walk last Thursday, I took a stroll on Friday, I saw the sights on Saturday, and I breathed the air on Sunday. I hate to do the same things over and over. It makes for such a boring existence.

Go to the store, look at the pretty women, mail a letter, but do something, Mr. Cherches, do something.

I went to the store on July fifteenth, I looked at the pretty women on September twenty-sixth, but I can't remember the last time I mailed a letter, Mr. Cherches remembers. Mailing a letter, that's how I'll spend my day. There's so much time and so little to do that new and unusual experiences make for an exciting existence. I'm going to mail a letter on this bright, sunny day. Hooray!

Mr. Cherches puts on his jacket, Mr. Cherches puts on his cap. Mr. Cherches leaves his apartment and greets the day. It is a bright, sunny day. Mr. Sun smiles at Mr. Cherches. Mr. Cherches smiles at Mr. Sun.

It is such a nice day that Mr. Cherches begins to sing:

> I'm going to mail a letter,
>
> I'm going to mail a letter,
>
> Things could be no better,
>
> I'm a real go-getter,
>
> It's a bright, sunny day,
>
> And I hope it stays that way,
>
> 'Cause I'm going to mail a letter today, hey-hey,
>
> I'm going to mail a letter today.

Mr. Cherches walks down the block until he reaches a mailbox. Mr. Cherches is going to mail a letter. Mr. Cherches is going to drop a letter in the mailbox. This is the climax of his day.

But wait! There's a problem—Mr. Cherches has neglected one important detail—he doesn't have a letter to mail.

Mr. Cherches, Mr. Cherches, one cannot mail a letter unless one has a letter to mail.

Can it be true? Mr. Cherches wonders. Does one really need to have a letter to mail before one can mail a letter?

It sounds logical, but what will I do now?

Write a letter, Mr. Cherches, write a letter.

I guess that's what I'll have to do, Mr. Cherches guesses, I guess I'll have to write a letter. So he rushes home to write a letter, to write a letter to mail.

To whom should I write a letter? Mr. Cherches wonders. I can't write a letter to a friend, that would be silly, I don't have any friends. I can't write a fan letter, there's nobody I want to write a fan letter to. I can't write a letter of complaint, it's a bright, sunny day, and one should never write a letter of complaint on a bright, sunny day, one should always save letters of complaint for dark, gloomy days. I guess I'll just have to write a letter to myself.

So Mr. Cherches writes a letter to himself.

Dear Mr. Cherches,

I am writing you this letter because I need to write a letter so I can have a letter to mail. I decided to mail a letter today, but when I got to the mailbox I discovered that I did not have a letter to mail. This was bad news, because in order to mail a letter you have to have a letter to mail. So I rushed home in order to write this letter to you so I would have a letter to mail. But you already know this because you are me.

Respectfully,
Mr. Cherches

Mr. Cherches signs the letter. He folds it and places it in an envelope. He seals the envelope. He writes his own address on it. He puts a stamp on it. The letter is all ready to be mailed. Oh boy!

But wait, Mr. Cherches, take a look out the window.

Mr. Cherches looks out the window. Oh no, it's raining!

That's right, Mr. Cherches, the weatherman is playing a trick on you. It's raining outside, and one should never go out in the rain to mail a letter. You're just going to have to call the whole thing off.

Mr. Cherches begins to cry. It is raining outside, and now I won't be able to mail my letter, he thinks. My whole day is ruined.

Don't take it so hard, Mr. Cherches, look on the bright side of things. You've already had quite a busy day. You went out to mail a letter, a noble effort in itself, and when you discovered that you did not have a letter to mail, did you accept defeat? Of course not, you went home and wrote a letter, and quite a good one at that. And now you have a letter all ready to mail tomorrow. So things have actually worked out quite nicely.

It's true, Mr. Cherches tells himself. I have had quite an exciting day. And not only has today been taken care of, I also have my tomorrow all cut out for me. There's so much time and so little to do; it's oh so comforting to know that, should I still be alive, there's something new and exciting for me to do tomorrow.

And Mr. Cherches begins to sing:

I'll mail my letter tomorrow,
I'll mail my letter tomorrow,
I've got no cause for sorrow,
I've got no cause for sorrow,
There's so much time and so little to do,
But I've got something to do tomorrow,
Something to do tomorrow...

# MR. CHERCHES GOES TO MARS

"Congratulations! You are the winner of a one-week, all-expense-paid trip to Mars," the letter read.

Mr. Cherches remembered that he had entered the "Trip to Mars Contest" several months earlier. There was an entry form on the back of a box of his favorite breakfast cereal, Planet Puffs 'N' Stuff. On the box it said: "Be the first person to visit Mars! Send us this original entry form or a reasonable facsimile." Since Mr. Cherches wasn't sure what a reasonable facsimile was, he sent the original.

And now he was the winner!

The rocket was scheduled to leave Earth in two days. Mr. Cherches had a lot to do to get ready. He had to do his laundry, he had to find somebody to water his plants while he was away, and he had to buy a travel toothbrush.

\* \* \*

Two days later Mr. Cherches arrived in Cape Canaveral for his flight to Mars. As he entered the spaceship, he was greeted by the pilot. "Hello, my name is Captain Singh," said the pilot. "Please watch your step as you board the rocket."

This is so exciting! Mr. Cherches thought.

Mr. Cherches settled in and Captain Singh took off. There were just the two of them on the rocket.

After they had been in space for a while, Mr. Cherches experienced weightlessness for the first time. It felt pretty strange. It must be an acquired taste, he thought. Mr. Cherches was glad he hadn't gone on a diet before the flight. Weightlessness felt weird enough. He didn't want to know what weightlessness minus five pounds felt like.

"Have something to eat," Captain Singh said as he handed Mr. Cherches a tube of space food. "It's going to be a long flight."

Mr. Cherches took a taste of the food. It tasted very familiar. That's because it was a paste of mashed up Planet Puffs 'N' Stuff mixed with milk. Even though Mr. Cherches loved a nice bowl of Planet Puffs 'N' Stuff with cold milk every morning, it was no fun if you couldn't see the planets. Besides, he found the thick, warm paste a little sickening. "Is there anything else to eat?" Mr. Cherches asked.

"I'm afraid not," said Captain Singh. "Planet Puffs 'N' Stuff Paste is all we have for the entire trip."

Mr. Cherches hoped the food on Mars would be better.

A few hours later, Mr. Cherches looked out the window and saw a big red ball floating in space. "Hey, is that Mars?" Mr. Cherches asked the pilot.

"No, that's a red ball," said Captain Singh. "We don't reach Mars for another week."

"Another week! But my whole trip is only a week," said Mr. Cherches.

"Don't worry, you have a full week to spend on Mars," said Captain Singh. "Travel time is not included."

A whole week before they reached Mars! That was a long time to be cooped up in a space ship.

Mr. Cherches was glad he had brought along a big fat book of "Mr. Cherches" stories to keep himself occupied.

* * *

A week later they landed at the Bradbury Interplanetary Spaceport, on Mars. "Have a good time on Mars, Mr. Cherches," said Captain Singh. "I'll be back in a week to pick you up."

When Mr. Cherches got off the rocket he saw that thousands of Martians had come to greet him. Many of them were carrying signs, which said things like "Greetings Earthling!" and "Welcome to Mars, Mr. Cherches."

A family of four Martians ran up to Mr. Cherches. "Greetings, Mr. Cherches," the father Martian said. "We'll be your hosts for your visit to our fair planet. It is a great honor to meet the first Earthling on Mars." Mr. Cherches shook the Martian's hand, which was green and slimy. "My name is XJ-R13, but you can call me Bud," said the Martian. "My wife's name is VB-B42-R13, but you can call her Maggie. And you can call the kids Max and Tiffany, even though their real names are YT-R13 and WZ-R13."

"Hello, Mr. Churchill," the children said, giggling.

"Pleased to meet you all," said Mr. Cherches.

"All right," said Bud, "we're off to the shelter unit! Zip zip!"

They all hopped into the extra-terramobile and drove off. When they reached the shelter unit, Bud parked the extra-terramobile in the two-extra-terramobile garage. Even though he'd never been to Mars before, Mr. Cherches thought the R13s had a very nice shelter unit.

"You must be pretty hungry," Bud said to Mr. Cherches.

"Actually, yes," said Mr. Cherches. "All I had on the spaceship was Planet Puffs 'N' Stuff Paste."

"Nasty stuff," said Bud. "We'll be dining shortly, and then you can have a proper Martian meal."

\* \* \*

At XJR o'clock they all sat down to dinner. Mr. Cherches was worried. What if he didn't like Martian food? He was afraid he might starve.

Well, Mr. Cherches had nothing to worry about. Maggie brought the food to the table and it smelled just great.

"I hope you like it," said Bud. "It's the planetary dish of Mars."

"Oh?" said Mr. Cherches. "What's it called?"

"Meat loaf," Bud replied.

"Meat loaf! Meat loaf is my favorite food on Earth," said Mr. Cherches.

"Well, meat loaf is our favorite food on Mars too," said Bud. "Dig in."

Mr. Cherches took a taste of the Martian meat loaf. "Wow!" he exclaimed. "This is the best meat loaf I've ever tasted. I thought my mom made great meat loaf, but this meat loaf is out of this universe."

"Glad you like it," said Bud. "You will never taste meat loaf on Earth that compares with Martian meat loaf."

"Why is that?" asked Mr. Cherches.

"Mr. Cherches," replied Bud, "I am about to tell you something that no Earthling has ever heard before. For thousands of years Martians have been visiting Earth. We travel in pairs, in flying saucers. When we arrive, we always disguise ourselves as humans so we can mix with your people unnoticed. We wanted to share some of the benefits of our advanced civilization, and we have given many good things to the people of Earth. We brought the Earthlings mathematics, medicine, soap, and the democratic form of government. Best of all, we taught the Earthlings to make meat loaf. But we didn't think the Earthlings were ready for the pure form of Martian meat loaf, so we left out several essential ingredients that make Martian meat loaf the best in this or any other solar system."

"What ingredients are those?" asked Mr. Cherches.

"I'm afraid I can't tell you," said Bud. "Those secret ingredients can never be made known to a non-Martian. That is the most important law on the planet, punishable by life without meat loaf."

Mr. Cherches decided that he had to find out what those secret ingredients were.

*　*　*

The R13s had a different activity planned for each day of Mr. Cherches' visit. His second day on Mars, Mr. Cherches went to school with Tiffany.

"Class, I'd like you all to say hello to our visitor from Earth, Mr. Cherches," said Tiffany's teacher, Ms. GL-H52.

"Hello, Mr. Churchill," said the class, and they all giggled.

"Now I'd like to begin our math lesson," said Ms. H52.

The class all paid attention as Ms. H52 read them the math problem. "Mother VB-M35-T88 is preparing meat loaf for her family. There are five members of the T88 family, two adults and three children. If a Martian adult eats 12 ounces of meat loaf, and a Martian child eats 8 ounces of meat loaf, how many pounds of meat loaf does Mother T88 prepare?"

Tiffany was the first to raise her hand. "Yes, WZ-R13," said Ms. H52, "do you think you know the answer?"

"Yes," said Tiffany. "Mother T88 makes 6 pounds of

meat loaf."

"And how did you arrive at that solution?" asked Ms. H52.

Tiffany explained. "Two adults eat 12 ounces each, which is 24 ounces. Three children eat 8 ounces each, which is another 24 ounces. Together that's 48 ounces, which is 3 pounds."

"Go on," said Ms. H52.

"But Mother T88 always makes enough for leftovers, so that makes 6 pounds."

"That is correct," said Ms. H52. "But how did you know about the leftovers?"

"Because the T88s are our neighbors," said Tiffany.

After class Mr. Cherches held Tiffany's hand as they walked back to the shelter unit. "I was very proud of you when you answered the math problem," said Mr. Cherches. "I would never have known that Mother T88 always makes leftovers."

"Thank you, Mr. Churchill," said Tiffany.

"By the way, Tiffany," said Mr. Cherches, "what are the secret ingredients in Martian meat loaf?"

"I don't know," said Tiffany. "Only full-size Martians know the secrets of meat loaf."

Drat! Mr. Cherches thought to himself. He felt like a worm for trying to wangle the secret ingredients out of a little kid, but he just had to know how to make Martian meat loaf.

*  *  *

The following day Bud, Max and Mr. Cherches went to the ball game. As they settled into their seats a food vendor came around. "Get yer hot meat loaf on a roll," he called out.

Bud raised his hand and said, "Yo! Three meat loaf."

The food guy handed him three sandwiches and said, "That'll be forty-two marsnitzes." Bud handed the guy a fifty and got eight marsnitzes in change.

Mr. Cherches couldn't figure out the game. The field had orange turf on which were painted what looked like random numbers. A guy threw a green basketball at another guy who held a big tennis racquet. The guy with the racquet swung and missed. Then he started running around the field like a chicken with his head cut off. A guy from the other team tackled him as the crowd cheered.

"I don't understand this game," Mr. Cherches said to Bud. "Could you explain it to me?"

"I'm afraid not," said Bud. "We can't make any sense of it either. We just come out for the meat loaf sandwiches."

While Bud and Max chomped on their sandwiches, Mr. Cherches ran after the meat loaf vendor. Mr. Cherches pulled up right behind the vendor and said, "Hey guy, I forgot what the secret ingredients in meat loaf are. Can you remind me?"

"Sure," said the meat loaf guy, "first there's—" Then he turned around so he could see who had asked the question. But when he saw Mr. Cherches he changed his tune. "Wait a minute–you're not a Martian. I could lose my job if I told you the secret ingredients. And what's worse, I wouldn't be able to eat no more meat loaf for the rest of my life. Now get out of my face!"

Curses, thought Mr. Cherches, foiled again.

* * *

On the fourth day Mr. Cherches went with Maggie to her office.

Maggie was a web page designer. She worked for the most popular website on Mars, allaboutmeatloaf.com.

Maggie showed Mr. Cherches around the office and introduced him to her co-workers. A female named GG-O22 shook Mr. Cherches' hand and said, "I've never met an Earthling before. I've seen pictures, but they're much better looking in person." Mr. Cherches blushed.

Maggie took Mr. Cherches to her cubicle. She logged on to the computer and brought up the All About Meat Loaf home page. All of a sudden Mr. Cherches smelled the most wonderful aroma. "Is somebody cooking meat loaf?" he asked.

"No," said Maggie, "that's the odor module you're smelling. All websites on Mars are odor-enabled." Mr. Cherches was glad Maggie didn't work for All About Bathrooms.

Maggie gave Mr. Cherches a tour of the website. "We

have a 'History of Meat Loaf' page, a recipe section, and a series of pages about meat loaf on other planets."

"Oh, is there meat loaf on other planets besides Mars and Earth?" Mr. Cherches asked.

"Of course," said Maggie. "Martian explorers introduced meat loaf to Jupiter and Saturn ages ago. We've tried to bring meat loaf to Venus too, but those Venusians are so primitive. All they'll eat is pot roast."

Just then a female voice came over the intercom: "VB-B42-R13, could you please come to my office. I'd like to go over the latest updates."

"That was my boss," said Maggie. "I'll just be gone a couple of minutes. Make yourself at home, Mr. Cherches."

This was Mr. Cherches' lucky break. While Maggie was gone he could look up the Martian meat loaf recipe on the website. He sat down in Maggie's chair, grabbed the mouse, and clicked on the "Recipes" link. When he did that, a box popped up that said: "Restricted area. Please enter password." Mr. Cherches didn't know what to do, so he typed some random characters and clicked "OK," hoping for the best. Unfortunately, he got the worst. A loud, screaming siren went off and all the lights in the office started flashing.

Maggie came running back to the cubicle, along with her boss and a security guard who had his laser gun pointed right at Mr. Cherches. "What happened?" Maggie asked.

Mr. Cherches was sweating bullets. He had to think of something pretty quick. "Ahem," said Mr. Cherches, "I was trying to get my email. I must have pushed a wrong button."

\* \* \*

Day five of Mr. Cherches' visit was Martian Thanksgiving. "This is the most important holiday on Mars," said Maggie. "We eat a big, festive meal and give thanks for all things Martian."

Mr. Cherches was looking forward to Thanksgiving dinner. All the food I've had so far has been amazing, he thought. This can only be better.

"I thought you might like to hang out with me in the kitchen and watch me prepare dinner," Maggie told Mr. Cherches.

This was better than Mr. Cherches could ever have imagined. Surely Maggie would make meat loaf for the most important holiday on Mars. All Mr. Cherches had to do was watch and remember the ingredients. "I'd love to," said Mr. Cherches.

"I usually start by preparing the side dishes," Maggie said. Mr. Cherches watched her make creamed corn, green beans, and sweet potato casserole with marshmallows. "And now for the main course," she said.

Mr. Cherches got goose bumps just thinking about watching Maggie make meat loaf.

You can imagine Mr. Cherches' shock, then, when he saw Maggie take a turkey out of the fridge.

"What, no meat loaf?" said Mr. Cherches, disappointed.

"I'm afraid not," said Maggie. "Thanksgiving is the one day of the year we don't eat meat loaf. It reminds us of just how thankful we really are for meat loaf."

What a gyp, thought Mr. Cherches.

* * *

On day six Mr. Cherches and the X13s went to the zoo. There were many strange animals at the Martian zoo. The only one Mr. Cherches recognized was the unicorn.

While the X13s were looking at the orangufrogs, Mr. Cherches saw something much more interesting. Standing a few yards away was a Martian in a chef's cap. I'll bet he knows how to make meat loaf, thought Mr. Cherches.

Mr. Cherches walked over to the chef. "Excuse me sir," said Mr. Cherches, "do you know how to make meat loaf?"

"Do I know how to make meat loaf?" said the chef. "Of course I know how to make meat loaf. Ain't I a Martian?"

"By any chance could you share the recipe with me?" Mr. Cherches asked sheepishly.

"Certainly," said the chef.

Mr. Cherches couldn't believe his luck. Perhaps the chef didn't know about the law against sharing the recipe with non-Martians. The chef recited the recipe while Mr. Cherches copied it down.

"Thanks," said Mr. Cherches.

"My pleasure," said the chef.

Mr. Cherches caught up with the X13s in front of the hippofoxbird cage. Mr. Cherches stuck his hand into his jacket pocket to get some nuts to feed to the hippofoxbirds. But when he did that, the recipe fell out of his pocket to the ground. Bud knelt down and picked it up. Oh no, thought Mr. Cherches, my cover is blown.

Bud started laughing uncontrollably as he read the recipe.

"What's so funny?" Mr. Cherches asked.

"I hope you're not planning to make this," Bud said.

"Why not?" asked Mr. Cherches.

"This is a recipe for animal feed meat loaf," said Bud. "I wouldn't even serve this to a Venusian!"

\* \* \*

On Mr. Cherches' last full day on Mars Bud said, "I thought you might like to go for a drive around the planet and see the sights."

"I'd love that," said Mr. Cherches. "Time has really flown. My visit is almost over, and I've hardly seen anything of Mars."

The whole family piled into the extra-terramobile for the scenic tour. Bud drove by the famous red sand beaches. They stopped at a forest that had the biggest, strangest, most colorful trees Mr. Cherches had ever seen. They saw the Red Mountains and the Very Red Mountains.

Then it came time to return to the city. Mr. Cherches had seen many wondrous sights, but nothing impressed him as much as the strip malls they saw along the highway. Alongside the various shops at the strip malls were dozens of restaurants with names like Meat Loaf King, Tip-Top Meat Loaf, and Colonel KF-C76's Martian Meat Loaf. All the meat loaf restaurants had long lines out the door.

"These meat loaf restaurants seem to be very popular," said Mr. Cherches.

"Best business on the planet," said Bud. "There's an old saying: 'Nobody ever went broke selling meat loaf on Mars.'"

"Which one has the best meat loaf?" Mr. Cherches asked. Max and Tiffany started laughing.

"The kids think that's a silly question," said Bud. "That's because all the meat loaf on Mars is exactly the same. There's no better meat loaf in the universe than the original Martian meat loaf, so there's no point in fiddling with the recipe."

When he thought about all those meat loaf restaurants Mr. Cherches saw dollar signs, and lots of them.

\* \* \*

Mr. Cherches couldn't sleep at all that night. He was leaving the next morning, and he still hadn't discovered the secret Martian meat loaf recipe. He just had to have that recipe.

In the middle of the night, as he tossed and turned, Mr. Cherches had a brainstorm. The X13s must have a cookbook with the meat loaf recipe, he thought. All he had to do was find the book and copy down the recipe.

Mr. Cherches snuck down, very quietly, to the X13s' kitchen. He brought his little travel flashlight with him so he could find his way around.

Just as he expected, on a shelf in the kitchen was a cookbook titled *Flavors of Mars*. Mr. Cherches looked through the book and found the meat loaf recipe. His heart started pounding. He quickly copied down the recipe and replaced the book on the shelf. Then he quietly crept back up to his bedroom. The rest of the night he slept like a baby.

\* \* \*

The next morning Mr. Cherches got dressed, packed his bags and went downstairs for his final breakfast with the X13 family. As usual, breakfast smelled great.

"You have a long flight ahead of you," said Maggie, "so I made you a nice big meat loaf omelet."

When breakfast was over it was time for Mr. Cherches and the X13s to say their goodbyes.

"Mr. Cherches, it was truly a pleasure having you as

our guest," said Maggie.

"Oh, the pleasure was all mine, I assure you," replied Mr. Cherches.

"We have been honored to be the first Martian family to host an Earthling–and such a well-behaved one," said Bud.

Then the kids spoke. Together they said, "We love you, Mr. Churchill!" That brought tears to Mr. Cherches' eyes.

"All right," said Bud, "before we get all weepy, I'd better drive Mr. Cherches to the spaceport."

And off they went.

* * *

When Mr. Cherches boarded the rocket Captain Singh asked him how he had enjoyed his visit to Mars.

"It was great," said Mr. Cherches. "Were you aware they have the best meat loaf in the universe?"

"No, I never knew that," replied Captain Singh. "It's the sad life of a pilot. I fly to so many places, but I never get to stay long enough to find out what they're really like."

As they took off, Mr. Cherches looked out the window and saw Bud waving goodbye.

Mr. Cherches didn't mind the weightlessness so much this time because he had gained five pounds from all the meat loaf he ate on Mars. When mealtime rolled around,

Mr. Cherches was happy to learn that the food on the return voyage was Martian Meat Loaf Paste. It wasn't as good as a real hunk of hot Martian meat loaf, but it sure was a lot better than Planet Puffs 'N' Stuff Paste.

As he was eating, Mr. Cherches' conscience started bothering him. "Hey Cherches, you're a real low-life," the conscience said. "You betrayed the trust of the Martians. You stole the secret meat loaf recipe, even though you knew your friends could get in trouble with the Martian law."

"I was very careful," Mr. Cherches told his conscience.

"Even so, it's the principle," replied the conscience. "You give Earthlings a bad name."

Mr. Cherches tried to keep himself entertained on the long flight home by reading a book he had picked up on Mars. The book was called *Mr. QB-R66 Goes to Earth*. While Mr. Cherches was reading, his conscience kept calling him names like "thief," "scoundrel," and "stinker."

Then, after almost a week in space, Captain Singh said, "Look out the window, Mr. Cherches" Mr. Cherches saw what looked like a toy globe. "We're almost home," said Captain Singh.

Fascinated, Mr. Cherches watched the Earth get bigger and bigger as they approached it. By the time they landed, Mr. Cherches had forgotten all about his guilty conscience.

\* \* \*

When Mr. Cherches got off the spaceship he saw the reporters and cameramen from all the TV news programs. The reporters huddled around Mr. Cherches and started asking him questions.

"Mr. Cherches, how did you enjoy your visit to Mars?" asked the first reporter.

"It was great," replied Mr. Cherches. "It's a beautiful planet, and the Martians are very friendly."

The second reporter asked, "Mr. Cherches, how does it feel to be back on Earth?"

"It feels great," said Mr. Cherches. "Mars is a nice place to visit, but there's no place like home."

Mr. Cherches took one more question. "Now that you're back on Earth, what are your plans for the future?" asked the third reporter.

This was Mr. Cherches' chance to make his big announcement. "I plan to open a chain of restaurants," he said. "Mr. Cherches' Original Martian Meat Loaf."

Then Mr. Cherches and Captain Singh hopped in a big black convertible limousine and drove off to the "Welcome Back Mr. Cherches" ticker tape parade.

* * *

Back on Mars, XJ-R13 and VB-B42-R13 were standing in their kitchen.

XJ-R13 was now certain that Mr. Cherches had stolen the meat loaf recipe. Mr. Cherches had carelessly replaced the cookbook upside down, so there was no doubt about what he had done.

"I knew we couldn't trust an Earthling," said XJ-R13, "but the joke is on him."

"What do you mean?" asked VB-B42-R13.

"I was sure that Mr. Cherches would not be able to resist trying to find the secret meat loaf recipe," said XJ-R13, "so I planted the false cookbook right here in the kitchen."

VB-B42-R13 looked horrified. "You don't mean–"

"That's right my dear," said XJ-R13, "the book with the recipe for the foulest-tasting meat loaf in the entire universe!"

# MR. CHERCHES GOES TO INDIA

"You travel so much, and you're a writer, so how come you never write about travel?" many people have asked Mr. Cherches. Mr. Cherches sees the question as indicative of the utilitarian strain in western thought. Experience is no good unless you can profit from it. Why not capitalize on the experience?

Mr. Cherches has never before written about travel because he has never had any idea of what to write, nor any desire to write it. He travels to get away from the other things he does. He travels for travel's sake.

Besides, Mr. Cherches finds the narcissism of most travel writing annoying—the incessant "I" angling for attention. Mr. Cherches can't decide which he finds more loathsome: the writing traveler who portrays himself as "representative" or the one who portrays himself as "extraordinary."

I have nothing to say about travel, Mr. Cherches thinks, nor have I come up with the proper angle from which to say it.

Nonetheless, Mr. Cherches decides to give it a try, as an experiment. He will write about his second trip to India, and he will write it in the third person. He hopes that will mitigate the narcissism of the "I." He will write scattered fragments that will be of no practical use to anybody.

In India, Mr. Cherches takes notes with ambivalence.

*   *   *

Recently, when asked what he looks for most when he travels, Mr. Cherches replied, "Foreignness." Of all the places he has been, India is, without question, the most foreign. The westerner in India is Alice in Wonderland: the rules of the game are not only different, they can't be fathomed.

In November of 1996, six years after his first trip to India, Mr. Cherches returned, spending one month touring the south.

*   *   *

His first morning his second time in India, at a hotel near the Bombay airport, Mr. Cherches peruses the room service menu. One of the choices is:

Indian Breakfast, Rs. 80.

Lassi (Sweet or Salted)

Aloo Paratha with Dahi

OR

Puri Bhaji

Tea or Coffee

Mr. Cherches orders sweet lassi, aloo paratha and coffee.

When the food arrives Mr. Cherches is presented with a bill for 105 rupees—there is an extra charge for the coffee. Mr. Cherches contests the extra charge and the waiter insists that the tea or coffee comes only with Puri Bhaji. Mr. Cherches had not realized the ambiguity of the first "or," though he does realize that he is now being charged more for a breakfast special than for an a la carte sum of its constituent parts. "Many guests are confused," the waiter tells Mr. Cherches, and Mr. Cherches figures the hotel is counting on just that. As he eats his aloo paratha, Mr. Cherches tries to remember the rule for "or" without parentheses.

*     *     *

At the beach in Goa, Mr. Cherches happens upon the following sign: DRUG OFFENCES PUNISHABLE WITH TEN YEARS RIGOROUS IMPRISONMENT. Mr. Cherches contemplates the possible meanings of rigorous imprisonment before moving on.

*     *     *

A Kashmiri shopkeeper in Goa stops Mr. Cherches. "Mister, do you know who you look like?" the Kashmiri asks.

"No, who?" Mr. Cherches asks back.

"Salman Rushdie."

Mr. Cherches does not know how to take this, but he

remembers an incident from his last visit to India. The first Gulf War had just started, and Mr. Cherches was checking into a Bombay hotel. The desk clerk, obviously a Muslim, on seeing Mr. C's American passport, proclaimed, "Saddam will bury you!" Mr. Cherches remembers having slept fitfully that night.

*       *       *

At the ticket counter of any railway station in India there is not an orderly queue, but rather a chaotic huddle of Indians, each trying to pre-empt the other, thrusting hands and voices at the clerk behind the cage. Surely Indians are the most incorrigible line jumpers in the world, Mr. Cherches thinks. Then he remembers some other places he's been. Mr. Cherches imagines a new Olympic event: the line jump. Without a doubt, India, China and Russia would take all the medals, though not necessarily in that order.

*       *       *

Indian soft drinks are served with the thinnest, softest plastic straws. You suck on them and they collapse. Drinking, like everything else in India, is difficult. Drinking a Limca, Mr. Cherches remembers a wonderful Raymond Chandler simile (from *The Long Goodbye*, he thinks): "He had a face like a collapsed lung."

*       *       *

Never wear sandals at night, in Kerala, if you're white, Mr. Cherches cautions.

Mr. C. had followed a lead on a restaurant in Ernakulam that specialized in traditional Keralan cuisine. The restaurant, Fry's Village, was an expansive outdoor place, set up like a series of traditional village huts. Mr. Cherches was the only westerner in the entire restaurant, and the mosquitoes had a field day. Here was a break from the usual, boring Dravidian fare—exotic American food (or, even more exotic, had they known, Russian Jewish food!). Mr. Cherches' enjoyment of his own meal of fish moily and kadala (a chick pea dish) with idiappam (rice noodle "string hoppers") was severely compromised by what had to be the two itchiest feet in Ernakulam.

*     *     *

"America—a fine country!"

Every Indian male and his brother, it seems, asks Mr. Cherches, "Where are you coming from?" It is not a question of perspective, nor of last place visited, but rather the Indian-English way of phrasing, "Where do you come from?" For some reason, the words United States or USA don't register immediately with Indians. There is always a pause, then recognition: "Ah, America!" So Mr. Cherches, no longer worried about being sensitive to the feelings of South Americans, begins to tell Indians he is coming from "America."

Sometimes, however, hardcore New Yorker that he is, Mr. Cherches will say he is from New York.

"Where in New York?" a hotel clerk asks him.

"New York City."

"Ah, not Long Island or Brooklyn?"

Mr. Cherches is impressed with the clerk's knowledge of geography. "Yes, Brooklyn," he replies. "But it's part of New York City. I didn't think many people in India knew Brooklyn."

"Yes, but I know because I am crazy for America," the clerk replies. "I know that Albany is your state capital."

Mr. Cherches is reminded of a little boy in Kathmandu, six years earlier: "I learn all about America at school," the boy had said. "I know Washington is the seat of your kingdom."

\*       \*       \*

After about a week of eating nothing but Indian food Mr. Cherches notices that when he sweats he begins to smell like a sweaty Indian.

\*       \*       \*

"Which way is Mahatma Gandhi Road," Mr. Cherches asks a man on the street in Trivandrum.

"Where are you coming from?" the man asks.

"America. New York City," Mr. Cherches replies.

"You are Jew?" the man asks.

Startled, Mr. Cherches thinks for a moment, then decides to say yes.

"I am Christian," the man says. "Do you believe in

Jesus Christ?"

"No," Mr. Cherches replies, then adds, "but I don't believe in anything."

"That is the way," the man says, pointing toward Mahatma Gandhi Road.

*    *    *

At the train station in Trivandrum an American with a vacant stare begins to chat with Mr. Cherches. The man explains that he has come to Trivandrum to see the dentist, but that he is living at an ashram several hours away. He then proceeds to bend Mr. Cherches' ear about his all-knowing, all-seeing divine mother. "She knows everything I did yesterday, and everything I did a hundred years ago, and everything I'll be doing a hundred years from today," he says. Mr. Cherches nods politely.

Sometimes, Mr. Cherches is amazed at how polite he can be.

*    *    *

Many people go to India to find themselves. Mr. Cherches goes there to lose himself.

*    *    *

On a restaurant menu in Trivandrum, soups are listed under the heading "From the Turin." This must be a typo, Mr. Cherches thinks. Surely these soups are not from the Detroit of Italy, home of the famous shroud, and of the great writer, holocaust survivor, and eventual suicide, Primo Levi.

*     *     *

On seeing Mr. Cherches' passport, a hotel clerk volunteers the information that his brother lives in Memphis.

"Do you know what Memphis is famous for?" Mr. Cherches asks the clerk.

"No."

"Elvis Presley lived there, and now many people make pilgrimages to his home at Graceland."

"I wouldn't know," the clerk replies.

Mr. Cherches decides not to try his luck with the song by Chuck Berry.

*     *     *

On the train to Kanyakumari Mr. Cherches is talking with a government employee on holiday. There is a lull in the conversation. Then the man points at Mr. Cherches' head and says, "You have lost your hair!"

*     *     *

Mr. Cherches phones the only decent hotel in Aleppy to make a reservation and gets a typically Indian commitment: "The room is reserved, but not confirmed." On arrival, Mr. Cherches is told, "We have no rooms left. Only a suit. Only a suit."

*     *     *

At a bird sanctuary in Kerala Mr. Cherches meets a local named Sebastian (there are many Christians in Kerala). Sebastian, an enthusiastic Kerala booster, is pleased that Mr. Cherches finds his state beautiful. "I welcome you to the land of lakes, latex, and letters," Sebastian says. "Letters because here in Kottayam district we are first to achieve one hundred percent literacy. And latex you know?"

"Condoms," Mr. Cherches replies.

Sebastian giggles. "Yes, condoms. And other things too. So welcome to the land of lakes, latex, and letters! You'll remember that? And my name?"

*     *     *

"Hello. Where are you coming from? America? Do you have American pen?" Mr. Cherches wonders: why is it that so many Indian boys and young men think that we foreign travelers come with an unlimited supply of pens to give away as souvenirs of our visit to their country?

*     *     *

Walking down the road in Kumily, Mr. Cherches meets up with three men, one of whom is carrying a boom box. They are listening to "We've Only Just Begun," by the Carpenters. Asians have the worst taste in American music, Mr. Cherches thinks, and remembers how often he heard Kenny G in China, and how he broke a little boy's heart in Shanghai by breaking the news that Karen Carpenter has been dead for years.

"That music is terrible," Mr. Cherches tells the men. "You should listen to James Brown, or Otis Redding."

"But we love the Carpenters. We love American music. We love Michael," one of the guys tells Mr. C. Walking down the road they converse. Two of the men are in their twenties and the other one is forty-five. The older one claims to be the grandson of the Maharaja of Travancore and is very drunk or stoned on drugs. It is 9:30 AM. "We are going to have a beer," one of the guys informs Mr. C. "Will you join us."

Mr. Cherches doesn't like the odds. Three Indians and me, he thinks, I'll be subjected to a constant grilling, have to answer interminable questions. It's too early in the morning. "Sorry, I never drink beer before 10 AM," he tells them.

\*     \*     \*

It's the phone system from another planet, Mr. Cherches thinks. There is no logic to the phone system in India. Sometimes the area codes have changed. Sometimes new prefixes have been added to existing phone numbers. But as often phone numbers are just swapped—for instance, a hotel's number is assigned to a private residence and the hotel is given a number that has been taken away from somebody else. Sometimes the new owner of an old number will have the old owner's new number handy, sometimes not. Sometimes a nonworking number will lead to a constant busy signal and no explanatory message, while sometimes you will get a message to "check your number." "Information," or "Phone Inquiry," if and when you can reach it, will as often as not have the old, obsolete number. One time Mr. Cherches got the following message: "The number you have dialed does not exist."

Don't visit India if you have a low threshold for frustration, Mr. Cherches advises.

*   *   *

Whenever Mr. Cherches phones a hotel to make a reservation and begins to spell out his name he is cut off by the voice at the other end.

"Yes, I know, Mr. Churchill."

*   *   *

On the train from Madurai to Tanjore Mr. Cherches wants to discard some banana peels and an empty drink carton. He carries the refuse out of his compartment and walks toward the end of the car. He sees an attendant.

"Is there a place to throw this?" Mr. Cherches asks, pointing at the garbage.

The attendant looks confused, perplexed.

"Trash. Garbage," Mr. Cherches says.

The Attendant, still looking quite baffled, points at the window.

*   *   *

There are many fascinating temples in Tamil Nadu,

both functioning ones and ruins. Mr. Cherches prefers the ruins, as he finds the practice of religion depressing.

*    *    *

At functioning Hindu temples Mr. Cherches constantly tries to dodge the greedy, relentless priests who follow him in a desperate attempt to impart some information in return for baksheesh.

"I don't want to know anything!" Mr. Cherches protests.

*    *    *

Indians will always refuse torn currency, but they won't hesitate to slip some in your change. Mr. Cherches saves torn bills to give as "tips" for "services" that he never requested in the first place.

*    *    *

India has a ways to go when it comes to politically correct language, at least as regards things medical, Mr. Cherches concludes, having passed the Hospital for Cripples and seen a bus belonging to the Spastics Society of India.

*    *    *

Nearly all Indian men wear mustaches. Many Tamil men are quite dark. Mr. Cherches notices a number of handsome men in Tamil Nadu who bear a striking resemblance to Billy Dee Williams.

*    *    *

In Madras Mr. Cherches passes a psychiatrist's office. The psychiatrist's name is Dr. Pannicker.

*   *   *

Indians tend to be a curious, loquacious lot. On countless occasions Mr. Cherches is asked his profession. He usually replies that he is a computer programmer. It's much easier than explaining that he's a writer of short, non-utilitarian texts.

*   *   *

On a tour bus to the Ellora caves Mr. Cherches sits next to a seventyish gentleman from Calcutta who had been educated under the Raj. When the man asks Mr. Cherches' profession, Mr. C., tired of saying computer programmer, mentions his part-time job. "I teach English," he says. "Writing and Literature."

"You teach Shakespeare?" the man asks.

"No, mostly modern literature."

"Ah, modern literature," says the man from Calcutta. "Somerset Maugham and Pearl Buck?"

*   *   *

At the Ajanta caves Mr. Cherches is being followed by a relentless postcard hawker. Mr. Cherches is sick of having his space invaded by Indians who won't take no for an answer. Exasperated, Mr. Cherches tells the hawker, "You should be more patriotic. Why don't you bother some Indians instead of foreigners?"

A young Indian man who has come on the same tour bus says to Mr. Cherches: "You don't like India, do you?"

*     *     *

Mr. Cherches decides that although India is easier, and in many ways more pleasant, the second time around, familiarity has mitigated some of the excitement of a first trip to India. What is missing? Mr. Cherches, rarely at a loss for words, has trouble explaining it, to himself as well as to others.

*     *     *

Most travelers who have been to India have a love/hate relationship with the place. Whenever Mr. Cherches meets others who have been to India the form of conversation is usually a trading of war stories, a mutual litany of complaints. Neither party has a good word for India, yet both invariably sigh and say, "I can't wait to go back."

# THE BARRY MARX TOUPEE
# STORY

My friend Barry Marx died at 41, way too young, in the middle of a phone call, of a freak heart attack due to a congenital defect he never knew he had. He was in L.A., living his dream, writing for television, something he had wanted to do for years.

I met Barry in 1978 when we were both students in the graduate creative writing program at Columbia, but I left after a year due to the stifling conservatism of the place. Barry was one of a handful of friends I retained from that year. We were both in the fiction writing program, but Barry's real aspiration was to write for film or television. He got his wish in 1996 or '97. For a few years prior to that he had been writing scripts for a video game company. It was when he worked as writer/producer of "Smoke and Mirrors," a Penn and Teller game, that he became buddies with Penn Jillette. I believe it was Penn who got him the gig writing for "Sabrina, the Teenage Witch." Penn also delivered the eulogy at Barry's funeral.

Barry went to movies all the time, more than I did, and when I saw him it was often to catch a film. This particular incident happened in the mid-eighties, at Manhattan's Paris Theatre, but I can't remember what film we saw that day. We had gotten there at least ten or fifteen minutes early and were chatting. At one point I told him about a guy I had seen earlier that day who had the most dreadful toupee. It was precariously perched atop his head, and though it was probably meant to be dirty blonde it was so dirty it was practically snot green.

"All toupees are lousy," Barry said. "There's no such thing as a good toupee. They all look phony."

"How can you be sure?" I asked. "A good toupee wouldn't look like a toupee, so you'd never notice it."

"No way," he said. "I'm sure there's no such thing as a good toupee."

We split hairs about toupees a little while longer and then moved on to other topics. Then the lights dimmed and the previews started. I don't think they showed as many previews back then as they do now, and pretty soon the film began. Shortly after the opening credits had run, only a couple of minutes into the film, four people from the row in front of us, two couples, began filing out. We both wondered what was going on. Had they decided so soon that they didn't like the film? Or had they already seen most of it and just wanted to catch the opening credits? We found out what was up soon enough. One of the guys leaned over to Barry, and in an incensed, menacing tone said, "Next time you feel like talking about toupees you're going to have to get yourself a set of false teeth!"

I could tell that Barry was shaken. "I had no idea there was a guy with a toupee in front of us," he said.

"You see," I said, "he had one of the good ones!"

# THE OTHER CITY

New York is a city of islands and canals. Known as the Venice of the New World, New York City is quaint yet cosmopolitan. The city is comprised of hundreds of tiny islands, and these islands are linked by a system of ferries which, while by no means perfect, usually function quite adequately. And while some of the islands are indeed self-sufficient, providing the inhabitants with all the necessities of life, and while some of the more well-to-do New Yorkers do own their own speedboats (there's no doubt they're well-to-do, as the cost of marina space is prohibitive to say the least), most New Yorkers are pretty much dependent on the ferry system.

Every island in New York has its own movie theater. New Yorkers as a rule are avid moviegoers. I'm no exception.

I don't keep a date book. Generally, I have a pretty good memory, but sometimes I screw up. It happened one day last month. I had made plans with four different friends to see four different movies on four different islands, all at the same time. And I didn't realize my error until the last minute, so I had to ferry from island to island to explain the situation to my friends.

The first island I went to was #46, which is fairly close to my home island, #42. My friend Marty J. was waiting for me in front of Cinema 46, where we had planned to see the latest Woody Allen movie (Woody, by the way, had grown up on island #42, and even attended my high school, #42 High). I explained the situation to Marty, apologized, and rushed off to my next apology. Marty C. was waiting for me in front of Cinema 62 on island #62. "I'm really looking forward to this film," he said. "Scorsese is my favorite director." I told him the bad news, said I hoped he enjoyed the film without me, and rushed off again. Cinema 130, a revival theater on island #130, had a double feature of "The Major and the Minor" and "Ace in the Hole." Wilder is my favorite director, so I was really sorry I'd have to miss this one. Anyway, when I got to the theater, Marty B. wasn't there yet. Marty B. is notoriously late, a habit that has always annoyed me no end. When he finally got there I told him what had happened, that I'd have to take a raincheck. I said goodbye and feverishly ran for the ferry, knowing that I was already late for my final apology.

At this point allow me to interject that there is one thing that does bother me about transportation in New York City. Although the ferries are relatively clean, and usually run on time, I am somewhat prone to seasickness. So by the time I got to island #302, which entailed a rather long ride, I was feeling a bit queasy. I did realize during my ride, much to my relief, that there was no need for a fourth apology, since I had already cleared my calendar of the three conflicting appointments. Well, at least I'll be able to see this new Australian film, I thought as I ran from the dock. By the time I reached Cinema 302 I was completely out of breath.

Andy had disapproval written all over his face. "The film's already started," he said, "and I hate to walk in in the middle."

"I realize it's my fault," I said, apologizing after all, "but do you want to do something else on the island as long as we're here?"

"I'll tell you something, Pete," he said. "I've been out of work for a long time and I'm getting fed up. You've been out of work for a long time too, and you should be getting fed up by now."

"What can we do?" I said. "There are no jobs in New York."

"No, but there are jobs in the Other City," he said and showed me an ad in the paper about jobs in the Other City.

The Other City is only an intercity ferry ride away from New York City, but it's like another world altogether, a teeming metropolis with nothing the least bit charming about it. The Other City consists of five boroughs, all linked together by a subway system and a number of bridges. The subway system is filthy, noisy, crowded and altogether unpleasant in ways too numerous to recount.

The ad was not very specific. It read: JOBS! JOBS! JOBS! Out-of-towners welcome, no experience necessary. See Mr. Moran. There was an address, but no phone number.

We took the ferry from island #302 to island number #110, where we made the connection to the Other City-bound ferry.

At the Other City ferry landing we got on the subway and took it three stops. The address in the ad was only a block away from the subway station. The sign on the building said O.C.M.T.S., and in smaller letters Other City Mass Transportation System. We walked in, asked for Mr. Moran, and were directed to a room where he would be speaking in a few minutes.

The room was filled with men of all ages. Just men, no women. Mr. Moran was a big, ruddy-cheeked Irishman. He spoke in a resonant voice with just a hint of brogue.

"Gentlemen," he said, "you're all here because you're in need of work, and frankly, we are desperately in need of workers, so desperate, in fact, that we are dispensing with the usual tests and requirements. All you have to do is say you want the job of subway conductor, and it's yours." The crowd of men broke into applause; some even whooped. "Now, for your orientation you will be required to ride every line of the subway system, from beginning to end, 24/7 for the next two weeks so that you'll be completely familiar with the routes. After that you'll be assigned a route and will work twelve hours a day, six days a week."

He went on talking, but I wasn't listening anymore. I just kept thinking, this job hasn't even started yet, and already I hate it.

# THE PASTA BREAKDOWN

I lost it at the supermarket, in aisle seven, pasta and rice. I don't know what happened; I just broke down. I was trying to choose some pasta. I wanted fusilli, and De Cecco is my favorite brand. But they didn't have any De Cecco fusilli. They had De Cecco ziti, De Cecco linguine, De Cecco spaghetti, and De Cecco rigatoni, but no De Cecco fusilli. The only fusilli I could see was Ronzoni, and I simply do not care for Ronzoni. I didn't know what to do. Was I more committed to fusilli or to De Cecco? Should I buy the Ronzoni fusilli in order to satisfy a craving for fusilli, despite my Ronzoni reservations, or should I choose an alternate shape from De Cecco? I wondered: how does one choose among ziti, linguine, spaghetti and rigatoni when what one really wants is fusilli? And then it happened. I started screaming, uncontrollably, at the top of my voice. I clutched my cart, which already contained a quart of 1% milk, a package of toilet paper, four cans of King Oscar kipper snacks and a Karl Ehmer Braunschweiger, and I began to scream a piercing, blood-curdling scream, crying at the same time, for I don't know how long. People were approaching, but also keeping their distance. "Sir, are you all right?" I heard. I still had the presence of mind to think, through my screams and cries, what a stupid question to ask somebody who is losing it. "Somebody call the police," I heard. "No, call an ambulance," I heard another voice say. "Call Bellevue," I heard.

A man in white, maybe he was the butcher or something, grabbed my shoulders. "Mister, please, calm down," he said. My screams must have scared him off, because he let go of me and backed away.

I couldn't really see, everything was a blur, but I could feel the presence of people all around me. Then came the words, my words, through screams and cries, "Get away, get away, get away from me!" People were scampering in all directions.

The next thing I saw was the hospital ward that enveloped me and a bunch of nuts, my ward mates, some giggling, some moaning. Great, I thought, I'm Olivia de Havilland in *The Snake Pit*.

I had apparently been given a sedative, or a tranquilizer—I really don't know the difference. I felt groggy, but otherwise fine. I remembered just about everything that had happened at the supermarket, up until I had, apparently, blacked out, but I couldn't figure out why it had happened. Pasta has never had that effect upon me before. A nurse noticed that I was awake and approached my bed.

"Mr. Cherches?"

Obviously they had gone through my wallet. "Yes," I said.

"Mr. Cherches, do you feel well enough to speak to a doctor?"

"I suppose so."

About a half hour later a doctor arrived. He looked like Leonard Nimoy. No, make that Martin Landau.

"Mr. Cherches?" he asked.

"Yes," I said.

"How are you feeling?" he asked.

I was feeling fine. "I don't know," I said.

"Do you remember what happened?" he asked.

"I started screaming in the pasta aisle, and then I blacked out," I said.

"Yes," he said. "We'll continue this later. We don't want to overdo it. Get some rest."

I wondered how much rest I had already gotten. My watch was gone. It was replaced with a plastic bracelet that had my name written on it, spelled wrong. My driver's license says Cherches, not Churches, damn it. I looked around the ward. There was no clock. I yelled out, "Yo, anybody got the time?"

The next thing I knew, three big, ugly orderlies were battering me with clubs, two more orderlies with bad skin and swamp breath were putting restraints on my arms and legs, a doctor with coke-bottle glasses and a hideous grimace was sticking a long needle in my right arm, and another doctor, a chubby dwarf, was sticking an even longer needle in my butt. All the while, Dr.

Martin Landau was taking notes and cackling.

Then, all of a sudden, poof, I was back in the supermarket, in aisle seven, pasta and rice. I was trying to figure out what kind of pasta to buy. They didn't have any fusilli in my favorite brand, and I didn't like the brand they did have. I began to wonder what would happen if, unable to make a pasta decision, I broke down and started to scream uncontrollably. I picked up a box of De Cecco rigatoni and put it in my cart.

# AT THE JAPANESE
# RESTAURANT

We go to a Japanese restaurant, myself and five friends. We all order the same dish, a mixed seafood salad. The salads arrive and they are quite a sight to behold– enormous bowls filled with seafood of all varieties: shrimps, clams, octopi, squid, salmon slices, fish heads, sea horses. There is only one problem, a minor one to be sure, but a problem nonetheless: there is one item missing from the salad of one of my friends, the man directly to my right. All of the salads except for his contain a rather large squid head, acting as a sort of garnish, in the center of the bowl. I call the waiter to the table, to alert him to this discrepancy. I explain the problem of the missing squid head and the waiter says, "I will correct this." I assume that the waiter will take the salad in question back to the kitchen and replace the squid head, but he does not do this. Instead he starts to shift food around from salad to salad, taking a shrimp from one bowl, a salmon slice from another, mixing the salads up in a seemingly random fashion.

"What are you doing?" I ask the waiter.

"I am correcting the situation by making all things equal," he says.

"That's not what I had in mind," I say. "You should be getting my friend another squid head."

At this point the waiter begins to get angry, raising his voice. "Are you telling me how to do my job?"

My friend, preferring to avoid further difficulties, says to me, "Listen, the squid head's really not that important to me. Why don't you just drop it?"

"It's a matter of principle," I tell him.

Meanwhile the waiter is continuing to mix up the salads, completely destroying the integrity of any individual salad.

"You're making a mess of everything," I tell the waiter.

"You think you know everything, don't you?" says the waiter.

"All I know," I reply, "is that five salads came with a squid head, and one came without it."

After a short silence the waiter looks me straight in the eyes and says, "One missing squid head! And to you that constitutes a majority?"

# BETWEEN A DREAM AND A CUP OF COFFEE

## THE DREAM

I went to a shoe store and bought a new pair of sneakers. My old shoes were in wretched shape, so I threw them out and wore the sneakers. I had the receipt in my hand when I left the store, and I looked at it. I won't need this for anything, I thought, so I tore it up and threw it away. Then I started walking. I walked for a long time, but I had no idea where I was going. I walked what seemed like hundreds of city blocks, some familiar, some not. After a while I noticed a problem with my sneakers: the stitching was coming undone—my new shoes were falling apart at the seams. I was distressed. I didn't know what to do. Perhaps I should return them and get a new pair, I thought. Then I remembered that I had thrown the receipt away. Now I couldn't return the shoes. And I couldn't go any further because my shoes were falling apart. I was stuck.

\*     \*     \*

I woke up thinking about the events of the day before. It had been a particularly odd day. First there was that crazy woman. And then that thing in the bank. And then the incident at the supermarket.

## THE WOMAN

The lines at Unemployment were longer than usual that day, and it took three hours just to sign. When I finally got out all I wanted to do was get home and take a quick nap. But first I had to go to the bank and get some cash. And I had to go to the supermarket to stock up on essentials. So I was on my way to the bank when this thing happened. An old lady, whom I had never seen before, came up to me and said she was my mother. She grabbed my arm and said, "Sonny, I've found you!"

"What are you talking about?" I said, wresting my arm from her grip.

"Sonny, I've found you!" she repeated.

"Who are you and what do you want with me?" I asked.

"I'm your mother, Sonny, don't you remember?"

"You're nothing like my mother," I told her.

She began to cry. "Sonny, you're breaking my heart," she said.

She was making me nervous. "Look, lady," I said, "I'm very busy and I've got to get going."

"Why are you doing this to me," she asked, still crying.

"I don't know what you're talking about," I said.

"I've been searching for you all these years—ever since you left me. And I've finally found you. Please come home with me."

She wanted me to go home with her.

I went home with her.

Basically, I was interested by this point. I wanted to see what it was all leading to. So we took a cab to her house. It was a big house, and I got the impression that she was pretty well off. It started me thinking. I'm on unemployment—it sure would be nice not to pay rent anymore.

But I couldn't go through with it.

"Look," I said, "I'm not your son, so there's no use in my staying here." And I started walking toward the door.

She was crying.

## THE BANK

So I went to the bank and another strange thing happened. I was standing in line and I saw a woman almost get her hand chewed off by the automatic teller. She had stuck her hand into the mouthlike drawer that delivers the money, to withdraw her cash, and the thing closed up with her hand in it. She tried to yank her hand out, but the thing was closed too tight. A couple of people ran over to help and tried to pry the drawer open, but it wouldn't budge. Finally, someone in line figured out how she could get her hand out: all she had to do was request more cash, and when the drawer opened up again she could remove her hand. So she pushed the button for another twenty with her free hand, entered her PIN, put her card in the slot, and when the thing opened up she withdrew her hand and her cash. Her wrist was throbbing and swelling. Tears were streaming down her cheeks. She picked up the customer service phone and started screaming at them, threatening to sue, and they told her she would have to put a formal complaint in writing. I wondered whether it was her writing hand that had been caught.

Anyway, when my turn came I took out fifty and then I headed for the supermarket.

## THE SUPERMARKET

I don't like supermarkets, but they're cheaper than bodegas, so I go to them when I have to stock up on essentials. But they always have the air conditioning up too high, they're always playing Muzak, and you're always bumping into people in the aisles. And this time, to add insult to injury, there was the thing with the nickels.

I had brought my groceries, mostly paper goods, to the checkout. The cashier tallied my items and the total came to nineteen-forty. I gave her a twenty and she gave me my change—twelve nickels. Would you believe it—twelve nickels! I couldn't believe it. You just don't do that with nickels. You don't go handing them out in bulk. It's not right. Nickels are too big. They're a necessary evil when it comes to small change, like to account for a five-cent denomination, but a whole bunch all at once? That's inexcusable. Nickels are big coins. Much too big when you consider what they're worth: five cents. Five lousy cents! A dime is worth ten cents and it's a lot smaller than a nickel. Dimes make sense, nickels don't. I'd guess that, speaking purely in terms of size, a nickel is roughly three times the size of a dime. Now does that seem right? A dime is worth twice as much as a nickel, yet in the same amount of pocket space it takes to carry around a nickel you can carry three dimes, which comes out to thirty cents. That's simple arithmetic. Or take a quarter. A quarter looks bigger than a nickel, but I'd say it's really not that much bigger because it's thinner. And besides, a quarter's worth twenty-five cents, so you can't complain about a quarter. But you can complain about nickels, and I did.

"What's the big idea, you giving me twelve nickels?" I said to the cashier. "Is this some kind of joke?"

"No sir," she said, "it's no joke. Your change was sixty cents. We had a surplus of nickels, and the manager told me I should give out as many nickels as possible."

"Well your surplus isn't my problem," I said, "so how about you giving two quarters and a dime." I gave her the twelve nickels back.

She gave me two quarters and a dime. "I'm sorry, sir," she said. "No harm was intended."

I nodded my head and pocketed the change. It felt right. Two quarters and a dime. Without a doubt the best way to make sixty cents.

*     *     *

I decided to get out of bed and make my morning coffee. I looked in the fridge and discovered that I was all out of milk. I hate to drink my coffee black, so I had to go downstairs to the bodega to pick up a quart of milk. I threw on some clothes. I was on my way out the door when the phone rang.

## A WRONG NUMBER

I picked up the phone. "Hello?" I said.

"Hello, is Ralph there?"

"No," I said, "this isn't his number anymore. It hasn't been for years."

I'm always getting these wrong numbers. Except it's the right number. That is, these people are calling my number, on purpose, for someone else. Always the same guy. Ralph. It's been happening ever since I moved in here. Ten years ago. At least once a month. I pick up the phone and someone says, "Hello, is Ralph there?"

The first couple of times, ten years ago, I figured it was just routine wrong numbers. Something close to mine, like maybe one digit off. But then I started asking. I said, "What number are you calling?" And they'd always give my number.

Ten years, and it still happens at least once a month. At first I figured maybe Ralph lived here before me. I'd imagine this guy in my apartment, picking up the phone. Then I realized that he probably didn't live here at all. They rotate phone numbers. Ralph lived somewhere else, but he had my number.

Sometimes they think I'm Ralph. "Hey Ralphie, how ya doin'?"

All these people, all trying to get Ralph after all these years.

Ten years, at least one of these calls a month. That's at least 120 calls for Ralph. Probably more, because the calls were more frequent at the beginning. Maybe more like 150–175 calls. And I don't think any of them are repeaters, because I always explain that Ralph doesn't have this number any more.

That's an awful lot of people.

Where is Ralph? Who is Ralph?

## THE BODEGA

When I got down to the bodega they were all out of quarts of milk. They did have pints, though. But pints were 80 cents and quarts were $1.40. Two pints would give me a quart, but it would cost me $1.60. One pint would do for the time being, of course, but then I'd have to buy another pint when I was done, and it would start a vicious cycle of pint buying. I'd be wasting loads of money if I kept buying pints. I could buy two pints now, just this once, and then start buying quarts again when I was done with the two pints, but I didn't want to spend $1.60 for a quart when I could get one for $1.40. But I couldn't get a quart for $1.40, because they were all out. Unless I went somewhere else. But I didn't want to go somewhere else because the next closest place was too far. So I stood there for a while, not knowing what to do. Finally, I decided not to buy any milk. I went back upstairs and had my coffee black.

# A Memorable Menu

I had gone to Chicago in 1986 with dancer Katrinka Moore and fellow writer Donna Ratajczak to perform our collaborative piece "Love Me Like a Bitter Pill" at a trendy club called Joz. Donna was a University of Chicago alum, and we stayed at the loft of some friends of hers in town.

The night after our performance we went out to a blues club with several of Donna's local pals. Another friend of theirs was the harmonica player in a band that was appearing at a club on the West Side. This guy had an interesting story. He had dropped out of a doctoral program in philosophy at an Ivy League school to make a go of it as a full-time blues harp player. Now he was living his dream.

Chicago's South Side is the neighborhood that's most associated with the blues, but the West Side has long had its own estimable blues tradition, exemplified by the late Magic Sam. At the time of our visit the South Side was a traditionally black neighborhood, but parts of it were racially mixed and much of it was gentrifying, for better or worse. The West Side, on the other hand, was the most notorious slum in town. Its residents were almost exclusively African American, and mostly impoverished.

It was an extremely high-crime area. In the danger department, the cliche New York analogy would have been the South Bronx. White folks rarely ventured to the West Side.

After a dinner of fantastic takeout ribs from Lem's (of the South Side), six or seven of us crowded into a car and drove over to the West Side. We spotted the club, which was called Purple Rain, presumably in honor of the Prince film, and parked about a block and a half away. It was indeed a blighted neighborhood, with burnt-out buildings everywhere you looked. As we walked toward the club several people on the mostly deserted street admonished us, in concerned tones of voice, "You folks take care of yourself around here."

The club was a ramshackle place that had the look of a Mississippi juke joint. I believe the club's name was hand-painted in purple above the entrance.

As we walked through the door everybody in the place looked our way. Except for two of the musicians, we were the only white people in the place, and at thirtyish somewhat younger than most of the clientele. A man with gray hair got up from a table where he was sitting with several other guys and asked us if we'd like a table. "I guess," someone said, and to our surprise he asked the other guys to get up. Then he got a rag and wiped the table. At first we figured he worked there, but it turned out he was a regular customer who just wanted us to be comfortable. I felt a little weird about displacing the people who had been at the table before us, but they didn't seem to mind. In fact, the whole time we were there people came over to ask us if we were doing okay, if we were having a good time. Everybody was going the extra mile to make us feel at home.

The featured performer was Tail Dragger, then completely unknown outside the West Side scene, but now a recording artist on Chicago's legendary Delmark label. Tail Dragger is a Howlin' Wolf protégé, and his moniker was bestowed upon him by the Wolf himself. Like Howlin' Wolf he sings in a gravelly voice, and that night in 1986 he worked with a wireless mike, at times slithering across the floor snakelike as he sang.

The guy who had cleared the table for us came over and introduced himself as Top Hat. He invited the women in our party to dance with him, and he danced with the grace one would expect of a man named Top Hat.

We all had a ball. It was one of those experiences you never forget.

Nor will I ever forget the menu. Purple Rain wasn't really a restaurant, but limited food service was apparently available. The handwritten menu hung behind the bar. It read:

M E N U

Ham Hocks
Hot Link
Boiled Egg
Alka Seltzer
Gum

# WORKING WITH FRANK

I had been working for Perdue for several weeks, but Thanksgiving would be the first day I'd actually be working with Frank himself. I was told to report to the big refrigerator at 9 A.M. sharp. I had never been to the big refrigerator before. My regular job was proofreading recipe labels. This was a special assignment. We were all expected to pitch in during the holidays.

When I entered the refrigerator I saw a short, fat, bald man. I went up to him and said, "I was told to report to Mr. Perdue."

In a voice that was unmistakable he said, "I'm Frank Perdue."

He looked very different than he did on TV—shorter and decidedly fatter—but the voice was that same nasal whine that had become his trademark.

"So you're the fella who's gonna be workin' with me?" he asked.

I told him I was.

"What do you usually do, young man?"

I told him.

"Well, you've been doin' a good job. I haven't caught

one mistake yet."

I smiled. There are few things more rewarding than being complimented on your work by the big boss.

"Well, are you ready to get to work?" he asked.

"Sure," I said. "What are we doing?"

"Haulin'"

"Hauling?" I asked.

"Yes. We've gotta haul these birds from the inner cooler—not freezer—I never freeze my birds—and we've gotta leave them by the door for the truckers to pick 'em up." He then went on to explain why we had to haul the birds to the door. Apparently it's a union rule. The truckers have it in their contract that they never go into the inner cooler, which is colder, actually just above freezing, than the rest of the refrigerator room.

So we went into the inner cooler and started hauling these big turkeys to the door. There were piles and piles of turkeys, and they must have all been at least twenty pounds apiece. And we had to haul all of them. Every last one. By themselves they're not too much trouble to lift, but after a while it's the cumulative effect that gets to you. And I have to admit, I was a bit out of shape. I found myself wishing I was back home, even if it meant a TV dinner for Thanksgiving. But I realized that Thanksgiving was a big day in the poultry business and I couldn't shirk my responsibility.

I decided to try to make some small talk with Frank, to make the time pass more quickly.

"Mr Perdue," I said, and he cut me off.

"Oh, you can call me Frank."

"Frank," I said, "I never knew we sold turkeys."

"There's a lot you don't know, young man," he said. "For one thing, these aren't turkeys."

"What are they?"

"These are my new big-breasted super-vixen oven stuffer roasters. Just perfect for those big family get-togethers, like Thanksgiving, Christmas, and Passover."

"I've never seen such big chickens," I said. "How do you do it?"

"It's done with a combination of genetic engineering and nuclear radiation," he said. "And the results are just scrumptious."

I was definitely taking a liking to Frank. He had a delightful way about him that you just couldn't resist. I felt so comfortable with him that I decided to be bolder, to ask him some more personal questions.

"Frank," I said, "how come you're doing this kind of work? After all, you're the president and founder of this company. You're the man on the TV commercials. Couldn't you get somebody else to do the hauling?"

"Young man," he said, "I'm a poultry man, and any poultry man who's worth his salt has got to get some chicken fat under his fingernails every now and again."

"Frank," I said, this time taking an even bigger risk, "how come you look so different on TV?"

"A simple video trick," he said. "They do it all with the vertical and horizontal adjustments." He was quiet for a few seconds; then he said, "Come with me."

I followed him to the room adjacent to the big refrigerator. It was a wine cellar. Well, not actually a cellar—we were on the fourteenth floor.

"Bet you didn't take me for a wine drinker," he said. "Bet you thought all I drank was Coca Cola."

I didn't say anything. He took a bottle of white wine from one of the racks and handed it to me.

"Here, take this garlic-flavored wine home and have a nice Thanksgiving dinner."

"You mean after we're done?" I asked.

"No, you can go now," he said. "I'll finish up myself. It takes a tough man to make a tender chicken, but that toughness has to be tempered with mercy."

I thanked him and thought to myself, garlic-flavored wine. Sounds interesting. Can't wait to see how it tastes.

# BLONDE LIKE ME

I had been advised to bring plenty of items that were scarce in the Soviet Union (which was really just about everything), to give out as gifts, tips, bribes. Especially important were packs of Marlboros. There was a serious shortage of cabs in Moscow and Leningrad (it was still Leningrad), and many people moonlighted as gypsy cab drivers. Flashing a pack of Marlboros was the best way to hail a cab. I also brought coffee, cassette tapes (for some music industry people I had introductions to), and hair dye.

The hair dye was courtesy of a friend who was working as a product manager for Clairol at the time. He had come up in the world, having recently left Ty-D-Bol and Cincinnati. "The women will love you," he said.

Back then the hotels had floor attendants, women who were stationed on every floor of every tourist hotel. Obviously they were there to keep tabs on the guests, to make sure Soviet citizens didn't come up to the rooms, and perhaps to make sure that only approved prostitutes gained entry. My floor attendant in Moscow was a chubby woman of indeterminate age with thinning, dreadfully bleached blonde hair. The first night in the hotel I unpacked my bags and brought a package of

Clairol hair color to the lady at her station.

"A gift," I said. "For you."

She looked at the box. "Blonde!" she exclaimed gleefully. "Like me!"

# EAVESDROPPING

We were having lunch at a Shanghai restaurant in Chinatown. Sitting at the next table was a Chinese man, dining alone, his back to us and his face buried in a newspaper.

"I just got called for jury duty," Masa, who is Japanese, said to me. "I'm not a citizen. How did they find me?"

"You have a driver's license, right?" I asked.

"Yes."

"That's probably it," I said. "In any case, they have ways of finding you if they really want to. It's a culture of surveillance."

At this point the man at the next table put his paper down, turned to us, smiled and said, "Culture of surveillance . . . I like that!"

# Jazz in Spain

When I was in Madrid I went looking for a café to take breakfast at and I passed by a place with a sign that said, in English, "Jazz Session." Being a jazz fan, I went in, though it seemed odd that they were featuring jazz in the morning. It was a fairly typical Spanish café, with a bar and some tables, but I didn't see a bandstand. Then I noticed a staircase with a sign that said "Jazz," and a red arrow pointing downward.

I walked down to the cellar and opened the door. It was a large room. The music sounded great. Better than I had expected. Rather than a small combo playing standards, it was a ten-piece group playing fairly complex arrangements. But the place was noisy with conversation. There were people in armchairs and on sofas conversing loudly. I hate it when people don't pay attention to the music, especially when it's so good. So I decided to get closer to the musicians. I recognized several of the players. They were major European jazz figures, mostly Italian. They finished the number they were playing and took a break.

A waitress came around during the break to take orders. I said, "Un café con leche, y..." I couldn't think of the name of the pastry I wanted, a little tart with almonds.

"Y-y-y-y-y," I continued, stalling. I figured even if I didn't know the exact name of the item I could ask for a pastry "con almendras." But I couldn't even think of the Spanish word for pastry. I was about to say "pasticcia," but that's an Italian word (and, as it turns out, a conjugation of the verb meaning "to make a mess"—who knew). I thought the word might be "torta," but in Mexico, at least, that's a sandwich. I didn't want to be laughed at for asking for a sandwich with almonds. The waitress was staring at me impatiently. I didn't know what to do. I wanted a pastry with my coffee, but I couldn't come up with the name. In one last-ditch effort to stall her, I said, "Y tambien..." When I said nothing more she announced that if there were no more orders she was leaving.

So I was doomed to having my coffee without pastry. And I was pretty hungry, too.

# RETURNING TO WORK

My first morning back to work after my vacation in Spain I took the elevator to the seventh floor, where my office, all right, my cubicle, is. But when I got off the elevator the floor didn't look familiar. Thankfully, I ran into someone I knew, from an old job, maybe twenty years ago.

"Rick," I said, "what are you doing here?"

"What do you mean," he said, "I work here." On the wall next to the elevators I saw a sign for the company we worked for all those years ago. How could I have missed that my previous employer was in the same building as my current one?

I told Rick about my problem, how I had taken the elevator to the 7th floor only to find a different company had that floor.

"We've had 7 ever since we moved from the previous location," he said. "Who are you working for now?"

I told him.

"Oh, they're on the eighth floor," he said.

All right, I thought, maybe I'm just confused this morning. I was a bit worried, as I'm usually on top of things, but I chalked it up to jet lag. I said goodbye to Rick, but not without first saying, "Let's do lunch sometime." Then I took the elevator to 8.

But that wasn't my floor either. It looked totally unfamiliar. Now I was really getting worried. There was a reception desk just past the elevators. I told the woman at the desk who I worked for and asked if she knew what floor they were on.

"I think they're on 6," she said, "but I'm not sure."

Well, I figured, couldn't hurt to give it a try.

I took the elevator to 6. It looked familiar. Like my floor. I used my ID card to get through the locked door. The office was laid out like I remembered, and I saw many familiar faces.

I got to my cubicle and everything was as I had left it before my vacation.

# Eudora Welty at the Supreme Court

I believe it was in 1989 that I visited the Supreme Court, spending a day watching oral arguments. I hadn't been to Washington, D.C. since I was a child. This time I spent a week breathing in American history and institutions. I visited both chambers of Congress and a bunch of Smithsonian museums, but the most moving experiences were a visit to the National Archives, a tour of the Library of Congress, and my day in court.

I had been fascinated by the Supreme Court for some time, especially from the perspective of its fragile role as protector of democracy. My interest had been further piqued during the Bork hearings, and I started reading books about the history of the court as well as biographies of individual justices and Woodward and Armstrong's *The Brethren*.

When the court hears oral arguments, there are two ways that John Q. Public can observe the proceedings. There is an express line, where visitors are shuttled in to a special section for ten-minute tastes. Those who want to stay for an entire session wait in a different line, and can remain for a full morning or afternoon session. One ought to line up about an hour in advance to guarantee a place, so I got there at 8 AM. The line itself was fascinating. Some, like me, had a general interest in the court. But others had particular interests in some of the cases being argued (two in each half-day session), and they illuminated the issues for the rest of us. It made the experience of watching the arguments much richer.

This was a time when giants like Blackmun, Brennan and Marshall still sat on the bench. Antonin Scalia was already on the court, and if I remember correctly Scalia was by far the most vocal and inquisitive of the justices that day, with Sandra Day O'Connor a close second.

During the morning's second case, I started looking around the gallery and noticed a face several rows behind me that was gnawingly familiar, but I couldn't put my finger on who it was. The face belonged to a little old lady. I kept looking back until I had an epiphany. It came in the form of a mental image of a TV screen with Eudora Welty sitting next to Dick Cavett, a scene I remembered from my own formative years as a writer. Yes, it was definitely Eudora Welty.

I love Eudora Welty's writing. Her sentences are musical, quirky and funny, and her writer's voice is unmistakable. Also unmistakable was her speaking voice, with its warm Southern drawl. In fact, when I was teaching creative writing I often used recordings of her reading her stories "Powerhouse" and "Petrified Man" to demonstrate the voice-page connection.

As we were leaving the court for the midday break I made sure I positioned myself to catch Welty. She was accompanied by a very tall, middle-aged woman, a striking counterpoint to this small, somewhat hunched eighty-year-old lady. As they made their way from their seats to the aisle I asked, "Excuse me, are you Eudora Welty?"

"Yes, Ah ay-um," she replied.

I told her how much I enjoyed her work, and that I had played those wonderful recordings of her reading her stories for my students. She was very gracious. She asked my name and wanted to know what kind of work I did and where I lived. We chatted briefly, and then I asked her what had brought her to the Supreme Court that day. Did she have an interest in a particular case?

"No," she replied, "I'm just here to watch our democracy in action."

Eudora Welty, in the flesh, was exactly as one might have expected.

# AT THE OPTICIAN'S

The right arm of my eyeglass frames had come off due to a loose screw, so I went to an optician's shop to have it fixed. The guy behind the counter, a young guy in his twenties, fixed it for me. Then he started writing something. It turned out to be a bill, on an official invoice form, for $3.95. I was surprised, because this is usually a free courtesy service, even if it's not your own optician. Nonetheless, I opened my wallet and pulled out a $5 bill. I was about to hand it to the guy, but I changed my mind, thinking, wait a minute, no way, this is a ripoff. "I'm not going to pay this," I said. So the guy snatched the glasses out of my hand. He took the screw out and handed my wounded frames back to me.

"This is an outrage," I screamed.

A man and a woman, somewhat older than the guy behind the counter, came out of an office to see what was going on. I explained what had happened. "Come with us," the man said, "and we'll try to get this thing straightened out."

I followed them back into the office. I sat down and the man opened a compartmentalized box that looked like a large box of chocolates. Most of the compartments had very expensive looking pens in them. The man pointed at each one and started giving me very complex and confusing explanations of what they were, none of which seemed to have anything to do with pens. I was becoming anxious and upset. "You're not giving me any context," I complained.

"Just bear with me," the man said. "Everything will become clear."

Then he got to another compartment in the box and I noticed that it contained a miniature white pistol. "Now you can become a junior secret policeman," he said, and handed me the pistol. "I trust none of this will go beyond these doors, Mr. Cherches." So, it's a bribe, I thought. Oh, what the hell, I figured.

"Don't worry," I said, "I'm not vindictive." After a pause I said, "Actually, I am vindictive, quite vindictive, as a matter of fact, but that's another story for another time."

I brought my glasses back to the counter. The original guy, that vindictive little twit, was gone, so another guy replaced the screw.

# ITALIAN DINNER

One recent evening I went out to dinner with a friend at an Italian restaurant, a local place, in my neighborhood, decent, nothing special, but friendly and reasonable. Because of its convenience I find myself eating there fairly often, and I pretty much know the menu by heart, so the wait staff usually ask, "Do you need a menu?" I rarely do. Anyway, this time I knew what I wanted, and I started ordering, but the word that came out of my mouth was not the one I had intended—I knew that even though I had forgotten the word I had intended to say before the unintended word escaped my lips. I said to the waiter, "I'll have the Risorgimento, please." I immediately realized my error. The waiter must think I'm a real jerk, I thought. But he nodded, wrote on his pad, and said, "One Risorgimento!" He took my friend's order, and then he walked toward the kitchen. I was sort of in shock.

Neither of us had ordered an appetizer, and after a while our dishes arrived. My friend's chicken Scarpariello looked pretty tempting. In front of me the waiter placed a large plate that was bare except for a fortune cookie in the middle. A fortune cookie?

I broke open the cookie and read the fortune: Without Risorgimento there would be no Italian restaurants.

# A CUP OF SUGAR

Someone knocked on my door the other morning while I was doing the cat-camel. I got up off the mat and went to answer the door. It was a neighbor, but I thought she had moved out of the building at least ten years ago. "Hi," I said. "I'm surprised to see you. Didn't you tell me you were moving to Berlin? That must have been at least ten years ago."

"No," she replied. "I've never been to Berlin."

Was I thinking of another former neighbor?

"But I haven't seen you around for at least ten years," I said.

"Well, I've been here all along," she replied. Was my usually good memory failing me? Yet she hadn't changed a bit. Surely after ten years she'd look a little different.

"Well," I said, "what's up?"

"I'm wondering if I could borrow a cup of sugar," she said.

A cup of sugar? Do neighbors still borrow cups of sugar?

"Sorry," I said, "I don't have any sugar."

"You ran out so soon?" she asked.

"What do you mean 'so soon'?" I said.

"Well, I just borrowed a cup yesterday," she said.

"That's impossible," I replied. "I didn't have any sugar yesterday and I haven't seen you in ten years."

"Very funny," she said. "Can I come in?"

"Why not?" I said.

She came into the apartment and went for one of the cupboards. She pulled down a box of Domino sugar. She poured a cupful into the measuring cup she had brought. "Thanks," she said. "I promise I'll buy you a replacement box." Then she left.

I looked at the box of sugar. On the bottom it said, in rubber-stamped lettering, "Best before October 2006."

Then I got back to my stretches.

# CHINESE MENUS

I love Chinese food, and consequently I spend a lot of time in Chinese restaurants. One of the fringe benefits of a meal in a Chinese restaurant, as if the food were not enough, is the menu. Chinese menus have some of the most remarkably odd locutions and typos. For instance, I go to one restaurant whose menu tells the customer that "the order of taking out is much larger than the order of eating here." Being a loyal fellow of the Order of Eating Here, I content myself with smaller portions. Another restaurant I frequent has a menu chock full of the most marvelous typos. Under the heading "Poutry" (no, there is not a section called "Prose"), they list an item called "Baked Squad." The seafood section gets equal time with two typos of its own. One item, nicely counterbalancing the squad, is "Fried Squib." And the other dish, which I have never ordered for fear it might turn out not to be a typo after all, is "Sliced Couch with Ginger."

# WING KEE

A stranger approached me and told me that I could save a life by visiting a certain restaurant in Chinatown called Wing Kee. Though I knew neither the stranger nor the intended victim, I accepted the mission, figuring it was my responsibility as a human being to protect the life of another.

I set out for Chinatown filled with a sense of urgency. I was not familiar with Wing Kee, nor was I familiar with the street it was supposed to be on, and I know Chinatown very well. I anxiously wandered the streets of Chinatown in search of the unfamiliar restaurant on an unfamiliar street. I knew that until I found the restaurant and went inside a certain person's life was in danger. I did not question how I could save a life by simply going to a restaurant.

Finally, I decided to ask for help. I went into another restaurant I had never been inside before. There were a couple of waiters up front. I asked them if they knew the street and the restaurant I was supposed to find. "Yes," they said, "let us show you."

We walked out of the restaurant, and next to it was an alley. At the end of the alley was Wing Kee. It looked like something from the fifties. It had a gaudy faux-pagoda motif and signs painted on the picture window in that old-fashioned pseudo-Chinese lettering. But what was most startling was the glow, like the glow from a U.F.O. in a fifties science fiction film. The glow flooded the alleyway. I started walking toward the restaurant. Halfway through the alley, enveloped by the glow, I turned around and took a brief glance back. The waiters who had shown me the way were nodding their heads, smiling knowingly.

# THE TRUFFLE PIG

Peter Wortsman and Claudie Bernard had invited me to dinner. Peter is a wonderful prose writer, a kindred literary spirit, and his wife Claudie is a scholar of the French novel. Claudie grew up in Southern France, but Peter, who grew up in Queens, always does the cooking, and it's usually something French. Whenever they have me to dinner I am a model guest, which insures repeated invitations.

They both greeted me at the door.

"Greetings, Pete," Peter said.

"It is so nice to see you," Claudie said.

"It's always nice to see both of you," I said.

I noticed something new in the corner of the living room. It was a big, grotesque, twisted, gray, headless carcass. But it wasn't a carcass. It moved. It shifted around a bit from time to time.

"What's that?" I asked, pointing to the thing in the corner.

"Oh, that is a truffle pig," Claudie said. "You know what that is, a truffle pig, yes?" she asked.

"A pig that ferrets out truffles?"

"I see you know a bit about truffle pigs," she said. "My mother, she shipped this one from home; she knows how much I love truffle pigs, and Peter and I had been wanting a pet for some time."

"But why doesn't it have a head?" I asked.

"You know, speaking of heads," Claudie said, "a truffle pig buries his head in the dirt and goes sniffing for truffles. When he finds one he brings it up and you have to get it away from him very quickly, because a truffle pig loves truffles very much. That is why truffles are so very expensive—they are rare to begin with, and the truffle pig eats many of them, so the ones that are left, they are very expensive."

"Yes, but why doesn't this one have a head?" I asked them again.

"Oh, it just came off one day," Peter said. "We keep the head elsewhere."

"Let's go to the dining room," Claudie said. "We will show you the truffle pig's head."

We went to the dining room and sat down at the table. On the table was a glass beaker that contained a small head, floating in a clear liquid. It was a very small head, in no way proportionate to the truffle pig body in the other room. In fact, it looked nothing like a pig's head. If anything, it looked like the head of a human fetus.

"And this is our little pig's head," Peter said, with a devilish smile.

"It is very cute, don't you think?" Claudie asked.

"Uh, yeah," I said, though actually I found the thing pretty repulsive.

"Pick it up and take a closer look," Peter said, "but be careful not to tip the beaker. Our little pig head is very mischievous—he likes to get out and crawl around the apartment sniffing for truffles, even though we all know there are no truffles here in New York City."

I reluctantly picked up the beaker, not wanting to offend my friends. I could have sworn the head gave me a dirty look. I put it down.

Peter served the wine, a very nice Macon Villages, and we updated each other on our work. Then Claudie brought out the appetizer, leeks vinaigrette. The beaker with the head was still on the table. It was making me a bit queasy, but I didn't complain.

Everything Peter served was delicious, as usual. The main course consisted of fruits de mer, sautéed and served in pastry shells, green beans, and baked new potatoes (I have always admired Peter's way with vegetables). For dessert we had fresh raspberries and cream. And I was the model guest, as always. I must admit, however, that I was rather uncomfortable this time, and in spite of Peter's wonderful cooking, and the stimulating conversation, my appetite was not as hearty as usual, what with that thing staring at me throughout the meal, making all sorts of faces.

# NEW MANAGEMENT

There's a restaurant in my neighborhood I go to often, a simple café with good food and a welcoming atmosphere. I often bring a book, or an e-reader, and hang out for an hour or two. The staff all know me, though they don't know my name and I don't know theirs. Sometimes I stop in after I get home from work, but more often on weekend mornings.

I stopped in the other morning, and I expected everything to be as always, but when I walked in the door the place was completely different. The name was the same, but all the staff were different, the decor had changed, much more chi-chi, and the menu had been completely overhauled. It was now an expensive Polish-Vietnamese fusion place. Now anybody who knows me knows I rail against these unlikely culinary fusions. Why can't somebody just open up a good Vietnamese restaurant in the neighborhood? Why does it have to be Polish-Vietnamese fusion? Does anybody really need a kielbasa banh mi? And how had they made such a major overhaul so quickly? I was just there for coffee the day before.

Whatever. I was about to take my usual table, or at least the new table that was in my usual spot, when a waiter came over to me. He looked Asian, but he was wearing a name tag that said Casimir. "Do you have a reservation, Sir?" he asked.

"No," I said. As far as I knew they never took reservations before.

"Oh, I'm so sorry," Casimir told me, "we're all booked up."

It was 10am and the place was three-quarters empty.

"But there's nobody here," I said. "I just want to have my usual cup of coffee, and maybe a scone or a croissant."

"Sorry," he said, "we don't have scones or croissants, only dinner plates."

"But it's 10am," I said. "Who's going to eat dinner?"

"It's 4pm in Warsaw," Casimir replied. "The early diners will be arriving shortly."

So I left and went elsewhere.

Don't you hate it when a place you really love changes hands and messes with a good thing?

# MY NEW NEIGHBOR

I was trying to sleep in, but somebody rang my bell at 7:30. I got up, threw on a robe, and went to the door, figuring it must be a neighbor since nobody had rung the downstairs buzzer. I opened the door and to my surprise a large fish was standing there. "Excuse me," he said (the voice was masculine), "I'm your new neighbor from across the hall. My bathroom is being renovated, and I was wondering if I could borrow your bathtub."

"Well," I said, "I'm sorry about your trouble, but I'm trying to get a little more sleep, and I don't think I can help you out."

"Please," he said. "I'm a fish out of water. If I stay dry much longer I'll die."

With a plea like that I certainly couldn't turn him down, could I? But he's been in the tub all day, and the bastard has me waiting on him hand and foot, or should I say fin and tail, in my own damn apartment. "Well, I certainly can't get out of the tub and get it myself," he whines, of the shrimp he discovered I have in the freezer. "Can I?"

# DINNER MUSIC, OF SORTS

Gyeongju closes early. I ventured out a little before 8PM to the restaurant area nearest my guest house, as I didn't feel like taking the further walk to downtown Gyeongju, especially since the restaurant pickings in that area didn't seem any more remarkable.

Already a number of places were closed, and I was thinking I might have to go to another area of town when I passed a place with no sign. There were a bunch of men, only men, inside, eating and drinking at traditional floor-seating tables. I walked in and took my shoes off. There seemed to be two groups of boisterous soju drinkers, one group behind a screen. I got the impression that this was a pub of sorts. I was greeted by a woman. "Menu? English?" I said.

"Menu!" she said, and pointed to the Korean menu on the wall. "Bibim bap?" she asked. I had quickly learned that's the first dish to be offered to Westerners, perhaps because it's an iconic Korean dish that's pretty easy to put together, and perhaps because it doesn't have the extreme flavors of a number of Korean dishes. But I didn't want bibim bap. I don't really like bibim bap. I figured I'd ask for Korean pancakes, since I'm always up for those. "Haemul pajeon?" I asked, hoping for seafood pancakes.

She smiled and nodded. "Haemul pajeon!"

"And a soju," I added. "Small." I made a hand gesture to indicate small.

Actually, I think all the bottles were the same size, about 12 ounces. Soju, similar to the Japanese shochu (though I find the Korean ones generally sweeter), is a kind of distilled grain spirit, often made from barley, that might be considered vodkalike, though milder, about 40 proof. Still, a small bottle of soju would have the alcohol content of about four bottles of beer.

My soju came and I started sipping. About a third of the way in I started getting a buzz. I was quite enjoying sitting there alone, sipping soju, taking in the social exchanges around me that I could make absolutely no sense of. Then my food arrived. "Haemul pajeon! Korean pizza!" the woman announced (indeed, it's cut in wedges). It was an excellent pajeon. I ate and I drank. About halfway through the bottle I was getting a serious buzz (I can't drink like I used to). I slowed down, but kept sipping. I wondered if women were welcome in a place like this, or if it was strictly a male preserve, as it seemed that evening. As a guy alone out for a bite, it was OK with me either way. In my soju-mellowed state I started focusing on the animated foreign sounds emanating from two groups of men in different areas of the room. I embraced it as an odd dinner music of sorts. About two-thirds into the bottle I called it quits.

# A LEAK

I woke up one morning to the sound of falling rain. But when I opened my eyes I saw sunshine peeping through the slats of the Venetian blinds. It wasn't raining after all. Then I realized the sound was coming from the bathroom. Damn, I thought, a leak from upstairs. I've had my apartment since 1988, so of course there have been occasional bathroom leaks over the years. But the current owners of the apartment above live out of town and only use it as an occasional pied a terre.

I got out of bed and walked toward the bathroom. The sound of dripping water was getting louder. Then I noticed a strangely familiar odor, or, more precisely, fragrance. It smelled a bit like gin, but no, it was something else. When I got to the bathroom I saw a puddle, but it wasn't water, it was an amber liquid, and more was coming down from the ceiling. Then I realized what it was. Vitalis! Yes, the men's hair grooming product that was very popular in my childhood.

How could this be, I wondered, a Vitalis flood? Do they even still make Vitalis? And who would have that much Vitalis anyway? I mean, the puddle on the floor of my bathroom probably had more Vitalis than even the largest-size bottle ever sold. And it was still coming down.

I threw on some pants and shoes and ran upstairs. I rang the doorbell. No answer. I knocked, repeatedly. No answer. Nobody home.

# THE STRIBBLE CIRCLE

Recently I started getting these very strange posts showing up in my Facebook news feed. They're from a Facebook friend named Jay Stribble, and they consist exclusively of strings of numbers, like 04023647. People sometimes comment on them. Sometimes the comments are also strings of numbers. For instance, Stribble will say 32323 and Stribble's friend Amanda Selwyn might reply 22223. Sometimes people do reply in words, but they're usually just congratulatory things like "Brilliant," or "I couldn't have said it better myself," which hardly sheds any light on anything. There was one comment, the only one that I found at all interesting, that said, "Have you considered a biopsy?" But that didn't shed any light on anything either.

Some of Stribble's posts get lots of "likes." And then again some don't. I have no idea why, for instance, 04023647 would get likes up the wazoo while 763985229 would totally bomb. I've thought of asking what it was all about, but I didn't want to look clueless among a group who were clearly cognoscenti of whatever it was I was missing out on. And another problem is I don't have any idea who Jay Stribble is. Luckily, it turns out we have only one mutual Facebook friend. That might have provided a clue, but unfortunately I don't have any idea who that other friend is either. I do, however, see that she and I have three mutual friends, all people I've either known personally or had other dealings with in the past. So which of the three mutual friends was the link to the friend once-removed from Jay Stribble? I could ask, I suppose, but would it matter? Would it explain anything? I doubt it. I'm guessing that Stribble friended me after I had friended or been friended by our mutual friend. Why, I don't know, but I'm guessing he wanted to expand the audience for his numerical pronouncements. And I can't deny that, however frustrating, there is something compelling about those strings of numbers. So I guess I'll just keep reading Stribble's posts as they come along, and maybe one day the light bulb will go on and I'll become a bona fide member of the Stribble inner circle. I'm looking forward to the day when I can read a post like 07634289502 and reply, "That just about sums it up."

# Berber Shows and Chickie Grills

When I was in Ho Chi Minh City, aka Saigon, in the mid-nineties, I hired a cyclo (bicycle rickshaw) driver on retainer. I paid him the princely sum, for cyclo drivers, of about $7 a day, to be at my beck and call 16 hours a day. He got me from place to place and took me on tours of the city. He was a poor, young guy from a village several hours away. He'd come into Saigon for days at a time to earn money to bring back to his mother in the village; he'd sleep outdoors, by his cyclo, near my hotel.

In most South Asian and Southeast Asian cities there are a range of private transportation options at descending cost levels: taxis, motor rickshaws (like the Thai tuk-tuks), and cycle rickshaws. In a few places there are even old-style rickshaws pulled by walking "drivers." I could never bring myself to engage one of those.

The bicycle rickshaw drivers are generally dirt poor and work for pennies. Rarely do they speak any English. It's a tough life. My $7 stipend to the guy in Vietnam was the equivalent of several days' earnings for scattered short hauls for locals. I remember once in Jaipur, India, I had asked a bicycle rickshaw driver the rate for a trip. "Cheh rupee," he said (six rupees in Hindi), about fifteen cents. He was amazed and effusively thankful when I gave him seven rupees. These guys don't usually get tips.

My Saigon driver did speak a little English, which is why I agreed to hire him for three days, though his accent was quite thick and he was very hard to understand. He was good-spirited and eager to please. As we were riding about town he'd point out things of interest, or presumed interest, to me. Since I was a guy traveling alone these often had a sexual angle, though it sometimes took me a while to figure that out.

At one point he pointed at a shop and said what sounded like, "Berber show! Berber show! Masa! Masa!" I had no idea what he was saying. Surely there weren't any Berbers in Vietnam, so what kind of show was he talking about? And what about Masa? I have a Japanese friend named Masa, and masa is the cornmeal base for tortillas and tamales, but he couldn't have been talking about Japanese men or Mexican food. It finally sunk in: he was saying, "Barber shop! Barber shop! Massage! Massage!" I had heard about these special "barber shops" in Asia. A guy sits in the barber's chair and gets serviced by the female "barber." Any hair that gets cut in the process is, I assume, only incidental.

Another time we passed a large public square. "Here, every night, chickie grill," I thought he said. I tried to make sense of this one. I had recently read about a street in Yogyakarta, Indonesia where at night hawkers sell fried chicken, so maybe he was talking about something like that. "Grilled chicken?" I asked. "To eat?"

He cracked up. "Chickie grill to eat! No, no, no!"

Somehow he conveyed to me that he was talking about prostitutes.

Chicken girl, I learned, is a term in Vietnam (and, indeed, much of Asia) for a prostitute.

# WHAT A ROOSTER CAN'T SAY

I must have been boasting or gloating about something, because Ida, my Ukrainian coworker, said, "You're crowing!"

A few minutes later I showed her a drawing I had just dashed off. It was a caricature of myself with a speech balloon in which I had written "Cock-a-doodle-doo!"

Ida looked at the drawing. "What's this?" she asked.

"It's me, crowing."

"But what's 'cock-a-doodle-doo'?"

"It's what a rooster says."

"What do you mean? A rooster says 'kukureku!'"

"In America, a rooster says 'cock-a-doodle-doo.'"

"Impossible," Ida said. "A rooster can't say doodle!"

# SOCIALIZED MEDICINE

I was strolling through a vast open-air market, like the ones in foreign countries, only this one was in Manhattan. There were numerous stalls, and the first one I stopped at sold Indian clothing. I said to the merchant, "I would like a sari—you know, one of those saris for men."

"Saris are for women," the merchant replied. "There are no saris for men."

"Well, maybe it's not called a sari, but it's like a sari, and it's for men," I said.

Another Indian man came forward. "Yes, I know what you are talking about," he said. "It is like a sari, and it is for men. We don't have any, but there is a store in Queens that might have some." He wrote the address on a card

I put the card in my pocket and went to the next stall. This one featured inoculations of some sort. The people in the stall told me that I had come at the right time, because they now had a new needle, much smaller and less painful than the old kind. The needle, they told me, was developed in a foreign country. Less painful than usual—that sounded good to me, so without hesitation

I allowed myself to be inoculated. The needle seemed rather long, but I didn't feel any pain.

Then I took the subway to the Indian clothing shop in Queens. I told the proprietor that the man from the market had sent me, and that I was looking for men's saris. He replied, "I know what you're talking about, but we don't have any. We do have some nice Madras shirts, however." I was disappointed—I had come for a sari, not a shirt. The shirts were nice, though, and I was considering buying one, but before I could make up my mind, I suddenly fell to the floor and scraped my elbow. There was blood—quite a lot of blood for a scraped elbow. I need medical attention, I thought.

Then I passed out and the next thing I knew I was in an emergency room, being attended to by a male nurse and a female doctor. The nurse said, "I'm going to give you a tetanus shot, Mr. Cherches. It's a pretty long needle, and it might hurt a bit."

"That's nothing," I said, and I told him about the inoculation at the market.

"No!" the nurse said, amazed. "That's a forty-five inch needle!"

"Oh no," I replied. "They had the new one—it's only fifteen inches."

"What are you talking about?" he said. "There's only one kind of needle. If there was another one, I'd know about it."

"It was fifteen inches," I replied. "They said it was from

a foreign country."

"Impossible!" the nurse insisted.

The doctor piped in. "He's telling the truth," she said. "It's very new. It was developed in Taiwan, and they're also using it in Cuba."

"I don't understand," the nurse said. "How is it that places like Taiwan and Cuba are so far ahead of us?"

In a combative tone of voice, I said, "It's because they have fucking socialized medicine!"

# COMMUNAL BOOK SHELF

In my building's laundry room we have a shelf for book trading. I went down to the basement one recent Saturday to throw away some stuff in the paper-recycling bin and I stopped by the bookshelf to browse. I saw a few titles I had left (books by Jo Nesbo, Oliver Saks and Evan S. Connell), a bunch of old travel guide books that are of limited value, about five Sue Grafton novels from the last half of the alphabet, an LSAT prep guide, and, much to my surprise, a signed copy of my own *Condensed Book*, my first full-length collection, from 1986. Now, I know I didn't leave it, because I just wouldn't have, but it was definitely my signature. However, the inscription really threw me for a loop. It read, "To Senator Hatch, with admiration, Peter Cherches." How could that be, a dedication to Orrin Hatch in my handwriting? I mean, I wouldn't even inscribe a book to most Democrats "with admiration." This really freaked me out. I thought about taking it, but I figured I'd leave it for a neighbor. When I went back with more recycling a couple of hours later, it was gone.

I hope whoever took it enjoys my writing. And I hope they didn't notice the inscription.

# Nightmare in Karnataka

The first two times I went to India I traveled alone. I love traveling alone. I think you can better get to know a place when you're not with somebody who's a reminder of home, and it also puts you in a better position to meet and converse with locals. My third time in India, however, in 1999, I traveled with Harold, an old friend and former neighbor. It was in 1991, I believe, that he moved to Minneapolis for a teaching job, and since then we'd arranged to hook up overseas on several occasions. He was happy to put himself in my itinerary-planning hands. I chose a route mostly through the state of Karnataka.

Shortly before this trip I had gone through a hellish six-month battle with insomnia. My doctor, a very thorough and cautious guy, sent me to all sorts of specialists to try to pin down the problem. After all physical causes had been ruled out he said, "I'd like you to see a psychiatrist." I was skeptical, but my doctor wasn't ready to prescribe medication, so I went to the psychiatrist.

The shrink, it turned out, much to my horror, was a classic Freudian with an inscrutable manner. His office had an analyst's couch. I explained my problem, and he proceeded to get my medical and family history. When I told him my father had died young he perked up. "How old was he?" the shrink asked.

"I think he was about forty-two," I said.

He didn't actually say, "Aha!," but I know he was thinking it. "Your father died at forty-two, and you're forty-two. Do you think that could have something to do with your insomnia?" he asked. He seemed thrilled by the prospect of a classic Freudian solution.

"Absolutely not," I said. "I don't remember him, I don't ever think about death, and I'm not particularly scared of it."

To make a long story short, I rebuffed his attempts to draw me into analysis and continued seeing him for prescriptions and follow-ups only. For some reason he was reluctant to try Ambien, so he gave me a series of prescriptions for drugs that were originally developed for other conditions, mostly antidepressants. One of them, Elavil, an old-school antidepressant that had been superseded for its original purpose by newer drugs, seemed to help. I was using Elavil as a sleep aid when I went to India with Harold.

Harold and I flew into Mumbai, then caught a domestic flight to Bangalore the following day. We were going to take the train to Mysore, which would be the beginning of a road trip that would conclude in Hyderabad (in the state of Andhra Pradesh).

At the Bangalore railway station we experienced a classic example of Indian bureaucracy. When we tried to buy train tickets to Mysore, about a half hour before it was set to depart, we were told that the train was all sold out. There was, however, a special tourist quota. A certain number of seats were set aside for foreigners. We had to go to the tourist quota office to see if we could get tickets. Otherwise we'd have to wait at least three hours for the next train.

Well, the office we needed to go to wasn't in the station. Of course not. It was in a shed about a quarter of a mile away, by the side of the tracks. We rushed over and entered an office full of female workers at desks and a single man up front at a bigger desk. Nobody said anything. Nobody said, "Can I help you." I figured the man was the manager, so I went up to him and said, "Excuse me, we're here about the tourist quota for the Mysore train."

"I'm sorry," he said. "We can't do anything now. We are all at lunch."

I couldn't believe it. The entire office had stopped working at the same time, and this guy wasn't going to help us make our train. I explained that this relatively simple favor would save us the trouble of waiting hours for another train, and reason eventually prevailed. We rushed back to the station with our permit and just barely made the train.

Mysore, which I had also visited on my first trip to India, is a charming city. We spent a couple of days there and arranged for a car and driver at a travel agency.

That was one advantage to traveling with a friend. We could share the cost of a car and not have to deal with getting around the state by public transportation, which can be slow and uncomfortable. Our itinerary would have taken us about twice as long by public transportation. Shared by two people, the cost of a car and driver is quite reasonable.

Karnataka is a fascinating part of India, with many architectural and archaeological wonders. Because the various sites are spread all over the state, however, it doesn't get much foreign tourism outside of Mysore and Bangalore.

In many of those off-the-beaten-path towns the best hotel is relatively humble. I can't remember the town this happened in, but our room had a lock that wasn't working, so the manager gave us a padlock and chain. I think Harold was still experiencing culture shock, something I had gotten over years before, and neither of us was thrilled with the lock situation.

We always shared rooms with twin beds. Invariably, the beds were right next to each other. In each hotel room Harold and I would move the beds as far apart as possible.

I took an Elavil and went to sleep.

At some point in the middle of the night I heard startled yells from Harold. "Huh?! Wha?!"

And then I realized that I had woken up screaming. I'd had a screaming nightmare.

"What happened?" Harold asked.

"I had a nightmare. I'll bet it had something to do with the drug."

"That wasn't just a scream, you know," Harold said. "It was a blood-curdling, other-worldly shriek."

I knew what he meant. I could feel the tightness in my throat. It's probably not easy to scream in your sleep, so the scream starts in the gut and works its way up, trying to force its way out, resulting in a harrowing banshee cry.

I promised poor Harold that I wouldn't take any more Elavil on the trip and hoped I wouldn't have another nightmare that night.

It was crude, primitive dream. My dreams are usually vivid and complex. This one was simple, but utterly frightening. I was an adult, wandering through the apartment of my childhood. Everything was in shadow. I couldn't see much. Nobody else was there. It was very quiet. I wandered from room to room, the air thick with foreboding. Then I entered the kitchen. All of a sudden an Indian with a turban lunged at me from behind the refrigerator, a meat cleaver in his hand. That's when I woke up screaming.

When I got home to the states I did some research and learned that screaming nightmares are a rare but reported side effect of Elavil.

# A Dream with Benigni

In my dream I was watching an opera on television. Already this was strange, as in waking life I'm utterly uninterested in opera. It appeared to be a nineteenth-century Italian opera. A pair of twins—short, fat, bald, dark Sicilian-looking men in Renaissance costume—were singing an aria in unison. I knew that they were singing about guilt, but I don't know whether this was because I understood the words or was familiar with the libretto. Then I realized that one of the twins had just realized that the other twin was not his brother at all, but rather a manifestation of his own guilty conscience.

At this point, Roberto Benigni, the Italian comic actor, appeared on stage singing the same aria. He seemed startled and upset by the presence of the bald twins. He made exaggerated comic gestures that signaled his fear, as if in a silent film comedy. He ran to the back of the set and hid behind a curtain, then peeked out at the twins with an ambiguous smile on his face. At this point I could tell that Benigni had realized that the twins were not real people, but rather representations of his own guilt. This liberated him to leap out from behind the curtain and continue singing his aria. The twins had disappeared.

The perspective in the dream then shifted from the stage set on TV to the room in which I was watching the program. There was another man in the room, sitting in a chair with his back to me. He was a large, bald man. I had no idea who he was.

"What am I feeling guilty about?" I said to the back of the man's head.

# A NEW YEAR

At 8:30 in the morning on New Year's Day I was awoken by a loud knocking on my door. Who the hell is banging on my door at 8:30 in the morning on New Year's Day, I wondered. I got out of bed, threw on some pants and opened the door. It was a South Asian man carrying a pizza. "Your pizza, sir," he said.

"I didn't order a pizza," I said, "and it's 8:30 in the morning."

"Yes, I'm very sorry about that," he said. "New Year's Eve and all that. Very busy."

"I understand that part," I said, "but I didn't order a pizza."

"Your name is Peter Cherches?" he asked.

"Yes," I said, "but I didn't order a pizza."

"Ah, but it says your name right here." He showed me the bill. "Is this your phone number?" Indeed, my cell phone number was on the bill.

"Yes, that's my phone number," I said, "but I didn't order a pizza."

"Please sir," the delivery man said, "it has been a very long night. The total is $18.50."

"But I didn't order a pizza," I said. "I don't want a pizza and I can't pay you $18.50."

"Sir, I realize you're upset because your pizza is eleven hours late, but if you don't pay me I'll have to make it up out of my own pocket."

"That's not really my problem," I said.

"Then whose problem is it?" he asked.

"I guess it's yours," I said.

"Perhaps," he said. "But I'm only out $18.50 whereas you, sir, have written a shitty story that has no point."

# How I Became a Circassian-American Writer

My family name, Cherches, is a Russian-Jewish name. My father's side of the family came from an area that I believe is in modern-day Ukraine, but for years I thought the name derived from Circassia, an area in the Caucasus. The Circassian people are known as Cherkess, and several academics, a classicist and a Near-Eastern specialist, on seeing my name and hearing it pronounced, posited that Cherches was a variation on Cherkess.

I had mentioned the Cherkess theory of my name's etymology on an online bulletin board, and a few years later a video appeared on YouTube about "The work of the Circassian-American writer Peter Cherches." It was wild. There was Circassian folk music and a caption that referred to me as the scion of one of the first Circassian families to emigrate to America. Then a man with what I guess is a Circassian accent read several of my pieces.

Where did this come from? I wondered. I figured it had to have been that comment I made online about the putative origin of my name. Somehow I had been transformed into a Circassian cultural hero, albeit a small-time one.

Eventually I did more research on the name Cherches.

I began to suspect the Cherkess connection when I learned that the people of Circassia, most of them now living abroad in Israel, Turkey, Syria or the U.S. are Muslims, and I could find nothing about a Jewish presence in Circassia. Interestingly, the Cherkess in Israel, though practicing Muslims, do not identify with the indigenous Muslim peoples of the Middle East, live peaceably with the Jews, and serve in the Israeli military.

Digging further, I learned that there is a village in western Ukraine whose Romanized spelling is Cherche, and it's smack dab in the heart of the region that so many Jews emigrated from, not far from Lviv. It seemed much more plausible that the family name Cherches derives from that place name than from the non-Jewish Cherkess.

But as a writer who revels in blurring the boundaries between fiction and nonfiction, as well as creating outlandish personae, I love the fact that someone went to the trouble of creating this biography of me, blissfully unaware that it was nearly total fiction.

UPDATE

*Shortly before this book went to press, I received this comment on the blog where this piece first appeared:*

Actually, your ancestors probably did come from Circassia. The original inhabitants were not Muslim and had many Jews among them. When driven from their homeland by Russians, many did settle in the

Middle East. But many Muslims were once Jewish. Also, the town in the Ukraine you mention was settled by Circassians. So there is nothing that contradicts being of Jewish-Circassian origin. I know this because I am a Cherches on my father's mother's side. Some of my relatives changed the name to Cherkes and Charkes, but in Belarus, from where they came to the US, they were all Cherches. The Circassian women were known for their beauty, and all my female relatives who took after my grandmother were beauties.

# Remembering Bart

We weren't really that close, especially in later years. He was 12 years older than me, and by the time I was 7 or 8 he was out on his own. But Bart was a formative influence on me in a number of ways. Since my father died when I was 2, my two brothers, both somewhat older, filled in some of the father-figure slack. Once, on an outing to Sam Goody's record store, ca. 1964 (a Beatles-buying expedition), a clerk said to Bart, of me, "He's a cute kid. Is he your son?"

A passion for music is one of the things I got partly from Bart. He was an obsessive record collector. Like our father before him, Bart was a big fan of the Great American Songbook and its interpreters, especially Sinatra and his crowd. As I got older we found mutual territory in jazz singers. But when I was younger Bart encouraged my burgeoning musical interests, sparked largely by the seismic cultural effect of Beatlemania, when I was 8 years old.

He was also an adventurous and enthusiastic eater. I first tried calamari on Bart's recommendation, at a local Brooklyn Italian restaurant. Back in the mid-60s calamari was not the ubiquitous menu item it is today. Back then it was considered weird or exotic food.

My brother was never one to do anything in moderation. Many of my earliest experiences of regional Chinese cuisines, in the early-70s, were in his company. Bart was especially excited by the newly available spicy Szechuan cuisine. One time he went to a Szechuan restaurant in Chinatown, Szechuan Taste, I think, and asked the waiter, "What's the spiciest dish you have?" The waiter named a dish and Bart said, "Give me one of those—and make it twice as hot."

Bart had a great sense of humor, which contributed greatly to his success in the sales game. The only reference I could find to him online called him "an icon in the insulation market for over 30 years." Styrofoam is a pretty dry product line, but Bart kept his customers in stitches with an endless barrage of jokes. Whether they were good or bad, he really didn't care. In fact, he had a real talent for delivering bad jokes. His wit could be acerbic (a family trait, I think). Once, at a rare restaurant outing with both of my brothers, in the late-90s, in Chinatown of course, I was reminiscing about the old neighborhood and our childhoods. I have a particularly acute long-term memory, and Harvey, the middle son, said, "How do you remember these things? You should go on Jeopardy."

To which Bart replied, "What would his subject be? Dysfunctional family trivia?"

# AN ARGUMENT

I woke up in the middle of the night because the neighbors were arguing. The walls in my building are very thin, plasterboard, sheetrock, whatever you call it. I couldn't make out the words, but there was plenty of passion, plenty of anger, plenty of noise. At 3am, no less. That's just not right. Consider the neighbors, neighbors. Consider me. But amid the incomprehensible cacophony of the argument I could swear I heard my name. Yes, several times. The husband said, "Peter Cherches" in an accusatory fashion. But the wife said my name in response as if it were the most ridiculous thing in the world. That was the last straw. I took a sleeping pill.

# THE STENCH

I awoke the other morning with the gnawing suspicion that I had fallen victim to an olfactory hallucination, if I might so characterize what I was then experiencing. You see, I had the sense of a smell I could not smell, an odor so unbearable that it would not, could not, reveal itself. Yet I knew it was there, somewhere. I couldn't smell it, but I was hyper-aware of the not smelling of it, this stenchless stench, and the knowledge was, in its own way, I suspected, as awful, as horrible, as painful, as the smelling of the smell itself would surely be, could I but smell it. This knowledge, as you might well expect, disturbed me for days. I couldn't sleep, could hardly eat, couldn't concentrate on my work. Nor could I decide which would be preferable—to go on plagued by this knowledge or to experience the odor firsthand and have done with it. I finally decided to put an end to this brooding, to name the smell and then forget it. The explanation had to be a convincing one, of course, so I considered a multitude of possibilities, finally deciding that the smell I could not smell was in truth a smell I hope I will never, in actuality, smell—the smell of my own death, or, more precisely, the smell of my own putrefaction, or, even more specifically, my ultimate putrefaction, that is if such a smell could be smelled from within, as if the process could sense itself, smell itself, know itself, until the sense consumes the smell, the smell consumes the sense, which is to say the self consumes the self, until the stench is none other than a smell unsmellable, a knowledge unknowable, which may or may not have been what I wasn't smelling, but for the time being, for want of a better explanation, it would have to do.

# BIRDS

I arrived in Phnom Penh late, just in time to go to sleep. I was awakened early the next morning by the sound of birds. But not just birds—perhaps the most beautiful chorus of bird calls I've ever heard, different birds, different sounds, all together. It was the best alarm clock ever, even if I'd have preferred to sleep later.

Throughout the day, around town, I heard the birds.

I'm sure Olivier Messaien, the composer who collected and reveled in bird calls, would have considered this the most sublime music.

Late in the afternoon I visited the notorious killing fields and the genocide museum, housed in the former detention barracks. As I meditated on the horrors I wondered about the birds, back then. In 1975, when Phnom Penh was forcibly evacuated in a matter of hours, did the city birds take notice?

And the birds at the killing fields: did they have any awareness of what was happening in their midst? Did they hear the screams and cries, or just go about their bird lives, singing their bird songs in blissful ignorance?

I know that birds grieve for their own. Do they grieve for us?

# Your Land Line is Dead

I canceled my land line about four years ago, but for some reason I never removed my old phone from the jack in the wall. I had completely forgotten about the phone until the other morning, when it rang. How could this be? I wondered, I've canceled my service. I picked up the phone. "Hello?"

No voice on the other end, just silence. "Hello?" I asked again. Still nothing.

I hung up. Must be some crossed lines or something, I figured.

I returned to what I was doing when the phone rang again. I picked it up. "Hello?"

Still nothing. "Anybody there?" I asked. Nothing. I hung up.

It didn't ring again until about two hours later. "Hello?"

Nothing. I hung up and unplugged the phone from the wall jack.

Then my cell phone rang. I picked it up.

"Your land line is dead," the voice said. I recognized the voice. It was a friend who had died three years ago, in a car crash.

"Jim?" I said.

"Your land line is dead," Jim replied. Then he hung up.

# THE RAVAGES OF TIME

I met Brian Olewnick in the late nineties as a result of overlapping musical interests. At some point in our friendship, maybe around 2005, Brian told me about his favorite LP, which he had bought in 1972, at age eighteen, when he was just becoming interested in alternative musical forms. The album was called "The Ravages of Time," and it was blank on both sides. Well, not completely blank—there were grooves, of course, but the grooves contained nothing but silence. Each side had a plain white label in the middle with nothing printed on it.

The album, Brian told me, was issued in a limited edition of only 100 copies. Brian felt extremely fortunate to have snagged one. The concept of the album was that with repeated listenings the "music" would change, that every playing of the recording would be different as the LP accrued skips, pops and crackles through wear, dust, and the other ravages of time. The only way to tell one side from the other, besides the aural evidence, was by the subtle aging differences of the plain white center labels. Over the years the music became much more complex, but for the listeners there were always memories of past states that contributed to the experience of the work—a palimpsest of aural memory.

The album became a legend in certain circles, and recently a record producer who is committed to aleatory forms decided to put the album out on CD. But, as every copy was different, very different indeed after more than forty years and different patterns of play, the question was which source to use. The producer eventually made the bold decision to put out a box set. He tracked down fifty copies of the album that were still in the hands of the original owners and transferred them to CD. Through a generous grant from a foundation that supports such projects, he was able to release the set earlier this year. In order to keep within the spirit of the original, each CD was unlabeled, and the set contained no liner notes and no information about the owners of the original source LPs.

The 50-CD set received mixed reviews. While some praised the attempt to document the music before all copies disappeared or became too difficult to find, most complained that freezing the music in digital form was antithetical to the intent of the work, that it was no longer vital, ever-changing, forward-thinking music. It was now nothing more than a "museum piece."

But for me it's something different, and wonderful in its own way. It may no longer be music that changes and surprises every time it's played—in fact, divorced from its original context it may no longer make sense to call it music at all. But for me it is now biography, a document of four decades in the lives of those fifty listeners—

interestingly oblique, intriguingly indecipherable biographies of fifty anonymous lovers of a certain type of art.

# COMPASSION

A man who looked like my mother with a mustache told me I must be on the wrong line. Isn't this the line for compassion? I asked. No, this is the line for luncheon meat, he replied. Well, then, where is the line for compassion? I asked. Let me see, he said, I think the compassion line is down that way (he pointed), between mustard and indignation.

I started walking toward mustard and indignation, but I could find no compassion, as the line between mustard and indignation turned out to be the one for bird calls.

I asked the guy at the end of the bird call line if he knew where the compassion line was. I think I remember seeing it when I was heading over here, he said, let me think. Oh yes, it's over there (he pointed), just past incontinence.

I didn't really feel like passing incontinence, so I waited on the bird call line instead. I waited 45 minutes and then my turn came. I was given the Swainson's Thrush. It was stunningly beautiful. As beautiful, I'd venture to say, as compassion.

# CODA

Pursue
Everything
Thoroughly,
Especially
Rest.

Come
Hither
Early
Risers,
Come
Hither
Evening
Stars.

# ABOUT THE AUTHOR

Called "one of the innovators of the short short story" by *Publishers Weekly*, Peter Cherches is a writer, singer and lyricist. Over the past 40 years his writing, both fiction and nonfiction, has appeared in dozens of magazines, anthologies and websites. His first recording as a jazz vocalist, *Mercerized! Songs of Johnny Mercer*, was released in 2016. He is the author of three previous prose collections, most recently *Lift Your Right Arm*, which Pelekinesis published in 2013. Cherches is a native of Brooklyn, New York.

CPSIA information can be obtained
at www.ICGtesting.com
Printed in the USA
FSOW01n1037220217
31106FS

9 781938 349560